After it Happened

Book 3: Society

Devon C Ford

D1607444

Originally self-published by Devon C Ford in 2016

Published by Vulpine Press in the United Kingdom in 2017

ISBN: 978-1-910780-28-2

www.vulpine-press.com

Dedicated to The Few.

The true friends, no matter how far away they are, who always showed their support.

You know who you are.

PROLOGUE

Maggie woke Cedric with a cup of black tea. She always woke before him, and their morning routine had begun to reintroduce itself. They were busy, and they were happy.

The twelve others who worked on the gardens would be coming soon, ready for a fresh day of working in the chilly sunshine. Cedric woke and smiled at her, pushing himself up in bed and squinting as he put his glasses on. She left him to get up in his own time and went downstairs to open the gates to their own walled utopia. She felt nothing was wrong as she walked past the rows of greenhouses.

Matty drove through the gates shortly afterwards, towing a benched trailer full of people.

They all greeted each other happily and Maggie laid out the plan for the day.

Cedric drank his tea and dressed, eager to join the others. He walked past the same greenhouses his wife had, without a care in the world. He slowed, his subconscious telling him something was different. He listened and couldn't hear the normal sounds of the morning. He couldn't place it, but something wasn't right. A shout: not a normal raised voice as people would do to be heard, but something in the tone that reached his ears made the panic start to rise in him. He stood still, debating whether to run to find his wife or go back and call for help. He didn't want to startle everyone by firing the fireworks alarm, but he felt something bad was happening.

Slowly, he turned around and walked back towards the house. His walk turned into a run, his fear growing every second until his shaking hands reached for the big pump-action Remington hung on the dining room wall. He kept it loaded so he just had to flick the safety catch off. He went back outside and heard more noises: a scream, another shout. He heard a single blast from a shotgun and ran to the garden. Inside the old lean-to garage, he kept a pallet of fireworks ready to go. He dragged it out, uncovered it, and lit the fuse. He didn't wait to see the bright rockets plume into the sky; instead, he ran to the road and turned right to cross the fields and get to the gardens from the rear as the sound of the rockets echoed and reverberated between the old walls. They were under attack.

HOSTILE TAKEOVER

Three of them were dropped off before the sun rose.

"Make me proud, boys," growled Billy from the driver's seat of the car.

They walked the short distance in and went along the wall until they crossed a field to climb fences and find a place to hide.

They waited for almost three hours until one of the ambushers heard someone walking towards them from inside the grounds. *There isn't supposed to be anyone here*, he thought, fighting his panic.

Failure was not something Billy liked.

He forced himself to keep calm and stay hidden, waiting for the others to turn up. A woman came into sight and opened the gates. *Good, they must be coming*, he thought.

A Land Rover drove in towing a big trailer. People were sitting in the back on benches. Lots of people. Including the woman, he counted thirteen of them, but none of them had weapons he could see.

They all gathered around the woman, who was telling them what she wanted them to do. He flexed his shoulders and gripped the evil weapon in his hands, preparing for action.

"Now!" he said loudly as he stepped out and levelled his sawn-off shotgun at them. The two others emerged similarly armed and took them all completely by surprise.

"In the shed, all of you. Now," he said.

They didn't move.

He stepped forward and drove the savage short barrel of the gun into the belly of a fat lad with a scared, round face. The lad doubled over, retching and struggling for breath.

"Now!" he said again. They started to move. "Where's the fireworks?" he yelled at the woman. She seemed confused, making him shout it at her again. Silently, she pointed to a box by a door into what looked like an office.

They filed into a large shed, where the other two began to drag the creaking doors closed. The woman began to speak, so he fired a single shot in the air. The noise was huge, and she didn't finish what she had started to say. The doors closed, shutting them in the dark.

Mission accomplished, he thought. Now to wait and launch the fireworks when the others were in position. He sat down, relaxing for now. He smiled, knowing that he had done his part well.

He leaned back in cruel satisfaction just as two dozen fireworks began to scream into the sky from the other side of the distant greenhouses.

DEAD ARM

Dan was awake, but he didn't dare move. Marie was asleep with her back to him, her hips and lower back pressed against his body. His right arm was under her neck and couldn't be moved without waking her. His shoulder was locked; the pins and needles were creeping up his arm.

He was happy. The rumour that she had been seen coming out of his room was a badly kept secret and was one that he refused to confirm or deny.

He heard the distant popping sound. It sounded like fireworks.

Fireworks, he thought. He hadn't heard fireworks in ages.

"Fireworks!" he said.

His bliss was burst like a balloon, and as he flew from the bed, he almost tipped Marie onto the floor, inviting a string of swear words from her.

She turned to see him throwing clothes on in a panic. Ash barked at him, also startled at the rude awakening.

"What the fuck?" she snapped, dazed.

"Fireworks. The alarm," he said, eyes wild with panic.

He ran downstairs, shouting at the others to wake up. A crowd ran from the dining hall, their breakfast interrupted, and he repeated his shout. He burst into Ops and threw open the armoury, loading his carbine quickly and shoving the ugly brute of a shotgun in the holster on his back. Steve ran in next, followed by half a dozen others. Dan looked at the CB radio. Nothing. He daren't try and call them.

"The gardens," Dan shouted. Steve said nothing and began to arm himself. A few minutes later, his Rangers were equipped and he faced the assembling crowd.

"The fireworks alarm from the garden was set off," he said. "Nothing on the radio to say it was an accident," he continued, pointing at the CB. "I'll go over and see what's happening."

He saw Leah and waved her towards him. "Fully armed," he muttered. "Get on the solar panel platform and cover the entrance."

She nodded and walked away, no fear in her eyes, only a grim determination.

"Neil!" he yelled.

"Here," came the call from over the heads of others.

"Get Thunderbird Two and mount the GPMG out front."

Neil nodded unquestioningly and left.

"Steve, with me. Joe?" he continued.

"Boss," said Joe from behind him.

"Clear the farm with Lexi. Stay on post until I call you back. Lex? Take a battle rifle as well and get up high."

They understood, but nobody moved immediately.

"Go," Dan barked, scattering them.

Calm yourself, he thought.

"What about me, boss?" asked Rich.

Dan thought that now wasn't the time to hold back.

"Kit up. Neil will be on the gun in front of the house, and Leah will be on a solar tower. Place yourself in the trees to the left of the road where you can cover them both." Dan stopped, grabbed Rich's shoulder, and spoke quietly. "Can you do this? If you aren't ready, you say so right now."

"I'm ready," Rich replied, the flash of steel in his eyes reminding Dan that this man had seen war and did not want it to come to his home. "I'm ready," he said again with pure resolve.

Dan believed him.

"Chris?" Dan shouted. He wasn't there; he was on the farm with Ana.

"Ewan?" he tried.

"Here," came the little voice from somewhere around the knees of the crowd.

"Everyone else who has been trained, give them a shotgun and some ammo."

Pete hefted his rifle and shotguns. "Me and the lad will be down by the lake," he said, waiting for no confirmation.

That was good, very good. If whoever was intruding knew this place, they would know of the small access road leading to the rear.

Please let this be an accident, Dan thought to himself as he strode outside flanked by Ash and Steve.

HOSTAGE NEGOTIATION

Dan forced himself to drive steadily, his eyes scanning for an ambush. Steve had also brought a heavy military rifle and had his carbine on his back. He loaded a twenty-round magazine, dropping an extra bullet into the chamber.

"Drop me short. I'll loop and come in from the back," Steve said.

"OK. Sit tight and do nothing until I do," Dan replied. He slowed down as they approached a junction, allowing Steve to slide out of the still-moving truck and sprint into the treeline. Steve would need maybe three or four minutes to get into position quietly, thought Dan as he rolled as slowly as he could to the entrance and turned in.

Nobody there. Definitely not an accident.

He got out of the car, leaving the driver's door open.

"Down. Stay," he growled at Ash. He wanted Ash hidden for now.

He walked slowly along, weapon ready but relaxed. He called Maggie and Cedric by name and only heard banging in response. They were shut in what they called the potting shed. He resisted the urge to open the doors yet, not wanting to fall for the classic come-on to put him in a kill zone. He waited.

If his opposition were trained, they would either be flanking him or waiting for him to make a move. If they were untrained, they'd be waiting for him to do what they wanted or expected.

He was sure he was being watched; his spine tingled with that familiar inexplicable sense. He stood still and waited. He saw a twitch of movement from the shadows of an open-fronted storeroom: undisciplined, moving position for comfort.

He decided to play on their nerves.

"Maggie? Can you hear me?" he shouted, loud and clear.

"Dan?" came the muffled reply and the sound of shushing.

"Yes. How many?" he asked.

"I saw three with sawn-off shotguns," she said, correctly anticipating the next question.

The hidden man's nerve-racked patience failed him. He emerged from the storeroom and walked towards Dan holding the shotgun at his waist. Dan looked at him, pulling a similar face to Ash's before he was let loose.

"What's your plan, boy?" Dan asked him.

"Shut up," he replied nervously, "guns on the ground."

He was still about twenty metres away, way too far for the sawn-off to do any serious damage to him.

"No thanks," Dan said, deliberately trying to unsettle him. "Let my people out and you and your two mates can go," he lied.

The man laughed nervously. "You'll put your guns down and join them."

Nothing like a bit of bravado to express how truly scared you really are, Dan thought. "I won't," Dan said. "You'll have to kill me, but you'll need to be a lot closer to do that. You ever shot anyone with one of those?"

The man clutched at his gun with sweaty palms. He hadn't ever shot at anyone with anything, and he was worried that this man in front of him had. Probably lots of times.

Dan saw a slight shadow of movement at the extreme distance of the gardens. Steve, he hoped.

If it was, he was in line of sight of Steve and his rifle. Dan turned and walked quickly to the building line before he sprinted around the back of the building and stopped behind the corner.

The man watching Dan's arrival had two choices: follow him or don't. One of his mates had gone to see where the fireworks had come from and hadn't come back yet. The other one was hidden on the other side of the shed where they had shut the others away. He chose to follow him.

He chose wrong and walked past the open door of the Discovery.

Dan watched from the corner of the building as the man's shadow crept closer. He timed it right, releasing Ash.

"GET HIM!" he yelled, hearing a snarl and a scream as he saw the shotgun fall to the floor.

He ran forward to secure the weapon and stop Ash from killing the invader.

Two things happened simultaneously. The man who had gone to check the house and the source of the unplanned fireworks came back after hearing the raised voices to see Dan at the corner of the building.

He crept up on this black-clad newcomer, and as he moved, the attacker raised the ugly gun to aim at the back of his head. He was about five metres away, close enough to decapitate Dan with a single twitch of his finger.

The other man hidden by the shed ran forward to help his friend, who was being dragged around the door of the Land Rover like in a horror film. As he stepped out, Steve saw daylight behind his target. No longer fearing hitting someone friendly, he fired.

The man aiming at Dan's head smiled, and as he heard the shot from Steve's rifle, he instinctively looked left.

Directly into the muzzle of Cedric's shotgun.

The man froze. He had no idea what to do, and there was nobody there to make his decision for him. He raised the shotgun, meaning to scare the old man.

The old man wasn't scared, and as soon as Cedric saw the man move, he pulled the trigger. The flame spreading from the end of the barrel was the last thing he ever saw as his ragged and torn body was flung backwards to slam lifeless into a low wall.

"Who's that?" Dan's voice called from around the corner, shaking Cedric from his entranced gaze at the dead man.

"It's me. Cedric," he said as he rounded the corner, shotgun held low. He saw Dan dragging Ash off another man who looked very pale and in obvious agony. A great lump of flesh was missing from his forearm, exposing fat and muscle. It reminded him of pictures he had seen of shark attacks.

"Maggie?" Cedric asked desperately.

"Shed, locked in," replied Dan as he got his dog under control. "Another one down further up. Come out carefully – Steve's down there with a rifle."

Cedric held both hands in the air, still carrying the pump-action. With less regard for his own safety than he normally would have, he moved into Steve's line of sight and rushed to open the doors.

He stepped over the last man, now lying where he fell with his arms in a grotesque pose, like a string puppet cut loose to fall to the floor. All that was missing was the chalk outline.

As the doors opened, Maggie threw herself into his arms.

Dan shut Ash in the Discovery and returned to the man on the floor. He slung his own weapon and picked up the sawn-off. Opening the breech, he found both barrels loaded. The man was whimpering where he lay, curled up, legs thrashing with the pain he felt.

No wonder, Dan thought; Ash had really taken a dislike to him. Blood loss was a concern, and he would probably never use that arm properly again. On the off chance he lived, that was.

"Don't go anywhere, treacle," Dan said with a worrying smile as he kicked the man onto his back. "I'm going to ask you some questions in a minute."

CHECKMATE

Billy and his boys rolled down the hill towards the house. They had seen the fireworks much sooner than he anticipated and waited for the cavalry to rush out and leave the main prize unguarded. They didn't disappoint him.

While the heroes were busy negotiating the release of their hostages, he would swoop in and take the house. Cruel, fast, simple and bloody.

I WANT A LAWYER

The man was hurting badly, grey with shock and blood loss, and shivering uncontrollably.

Dan dragged him to the front bumper where he sat him hard up against it.

Cedric had checked that everyone was unhurt and left them in Maggie's hands. She was straight on the radio to the house to let them know they were safe. Cedric came back over, still gripping the Remington. Dan looked at him, saw him shaking, and asked him if he was OK.

"Yeah, fine," he said unconvincingly.

Dan stepped closer to him. "Thanks. I owe you one. You did the right thing."

Cedric cut him off. "It's not that," he said angrily, then took a breath and closed his eyes momentarily. "It's not that," he said more calmly, looking directly at Dan. "I thought I'd lost Maggie." He closed his eyes again, letting the adrenaline wash out of his body.

"She's safe thanks to you," Dan told him softly.

Steve jogged up, having checked and disarmed his victim on the way up.

Dan saw him and nodded to convey his thanks for the good shot.

"Just three?" Steve asked.

"Looks like it. Let's ask," Dan said with a wolfish look on his face.

Dan turned to the pale man cringing against the front of his car. Dan drew his knife and cut a length of the man's top, making him flinch. He tied it tightly around his savaged arm as a tourniquet. "Don't want you passing out before you've told me everything you know, do we, treacle?" he said, giving him a less-than-playful slap around the face.

Dan stood. "Now. Who are you and why are you here, scaring my friends?"

"Fuck you," the man said through gritted teeth.

OK, try the hard man act.

Dan bent down to his face and spoke quietly to him. "Let's get something clear: there's nobody going to drag me away if I get too rough. There's no solicitor arguing for you. There's nobody to complain to. There's just us, and chances are if you don't tell me what I want to know, then you'll die slowly in a great deal of pain."

He stood again, receiving an angry stare through teary eyes. "Are you going to answer my questions?" he asked calmly.

"No. Comment," the man said, smiling through the excruciating pain as though he felt he had made a great joke.

"Very well," said Dan in a formal tone as he walked to open the door of the Discovery. "I'll give you a choice: talk to me, or talk to my colleague." With that, he whistled once and Ash bounded out of the car and stalked over to him. He circled around his owner's legs like a hunting wolf, never taking his eyes off the bleeding man.

"Watch him," Dan said, and Ash slowly stepped closer. Inches from the man's face, Ash gave him the full display of big, sharp teeth as he pulled his lips back and snarled.

"Watch him, Ash!" Dan shouted again, making the dog snap at his face and intensify the display with barking as he kicked it up a gear. "Good boy." Turning back to the man, Dan said, "Now, which one of us would you like to talk to?"

He decided to talk to Dan, who told Ash to sit.

"Billy gave us the orders. His 'dog' told him everything about you," he said in between gasps of pain.

"From the beginning," said Dan patiently. "Who is Billy, and how did his dog tell him about us?"

"We found him around Christmas. Wanted us to come and kill someone for him," he said.

"Who?" Dan asked impatiently, fearing the answer.

"You," he said, smiling through gritted teeth.

Dan turned to Steve in horror as the truth dawned on him. "Kyle. He's coming for the house," he said.

He considered putting two bullets in the wounded man's head, but he would have to wait.

"Cedric!" Dan bawled, running over to the rest of them. "Radio the house and tell them this was a diversion. Lock this place down and give those sawn-offs out." He turned and ran to the Discovery. "And tie this piece of shit up. Ash wants another word with him later," he yelled as he climbed behind the wheel. He reversed at speed, dumping the laughing man on his back painfully.

RAIDERS

Pete heard them first.

"Get yourself up there, lad," he said to James, pointing to a higher patch of ground ahead to his left. "Stay behind the big tree and only come out shooting if I shout for you."

James was white with terror but fought to control his breathing and find his courage. He nodded and ran, carrying a shotgun and cartridge bag.

Pete settled down on a large tree stump to look down the scope. He saw the two vehicles approaching and settled the crosshairs of his scope on the driver of the lead car.

He agonised over whether he should shoot or not. Everything told him that these people were coming to take what they had built. *Wait*, he told himself. *Wait*.

Neil had worked fast. With Rich helping, the GPMG was sitting ready and proud in front of the house in the bed of the truck. Nobody would risk driving straight up to it.

That made him pause. If they wouldn't come here, they would go somewhere else. Somewhere undefended.

He yelled inside for Ian. Jimmy poked his head out to say Ian wasn't there.

"Can you grab the keys to one of the lorries?" Neil shouted back. He told him what he wanted, and Jimmy didn't hesitate.

Leah lay flat in sniper pose: right leg cocked at an angle to allow her diaphragm to move without affecting her shot. She had taken a G36 which she had fitted with a bipod and scope for distance shooting. Nobody else used the guns, so they were effectively hers. She lined three magazines up by her left hand and felt for them as she looked through the optic, ready to reload without looking at what she was doing. Ninety rounds ready to go, and she would make them count.

She scanned the scope up and down the driveway, waiting as Neil called up to her to stay hidden until he fired first. She yelled that she understood.

Rich knelt behind a large oak tree. He was scared. Terrified, in fact, but the carbine felt good in his hands. He looked through the holographic sight, checking the approach road. He was to the left of the house, closest to the ones who had gone to cover the rear access track, a fact he was acutely aware of when a single gunshot echoed through the trees from where they were.

18

They had put all their best guns up front, leaving two civilians with hunting weapons to defend the rear.

Pete waited for the car to reach the narrowest part of the track with mud either side before he fired, putting a bullet in the driver's head. The car stopped, causing a pileup behind, as the others couldn't get past. The driver of the rear car tried the mud to the side and got bogged down as Pete hoped he would.

Pete racked the bolt slowly on his rifle, lined up again, and shot the second driver in the neck, seeing him flinch and grab at the wound, which now sprayed blood over the inside of the windscreen.

They realised that their element of surprise was lost, and they started to get out. They pointed in his direction and began to fan out. Pete slid the bolt with a smooth, practised action to load another bullet into the chamber, and vowed to take as many of these bastards as he could before they got him.

Lexi lay flat on top of a metal grain silo on the farm. Joe was below her somewhere, eyes on the road. She saw the three cars drive into sight. They didn't come to the farm but sped down the hill to the main house. She didn't have time to get a shot off, and had to make a choice.

"Joe!" she shouted.

"I'm here. What do you see?"

"Three cars heading fast for the house. I'll stay here; you move up to cut off the drive. Don't go in sight of the house, as you'll get shot by ours."

"Moving," was the only reply she heard.

~

When Rich heard the second shot, he knew he had to do something. He shouted for Neil's attention, but the older man couldn't hear him.

"NIKKI!" Rich shouted, using the abbreviated Nikita nickname as he usually did. He saw her scope swing towards him. He gave her three exaggerated hand movements: pointing to himself, then to the woods behind him, then a change of hand movement. He was telling her he was moving to flank the rear attack. Leah understood. She gave one flash on the torch attached to her weapon in acknowledgement.

"Go," she said to herself, "go get them."

~

The three cars raced along the drive, four hundred metres from the house. At three hundred metres, Jimmy did what Neil had asked him to: he drove the lorry forward and left around the ornate turning circle, exposing Neil with his legs braced wide and his hands on the machine gun.

Pete fired a whole magazine, killing three for the five bullets. He only had one magazine for the gun, so he had to load single rounds into the breech. It was quicker than trying to reload the mag. They were getting closer. He wasn't going to take them all down before they got to him.

Twice more he fired, missing with one shot. He thought of his girls, and a tear pricked the corner of one eye.

"Bastards," he growled. "Bastards."

He lined up on another, this time close enough to see the features of the target's face. He fell before Pete fired, his legs dropping like someone had switched his power off. They had. The twin reports of a double-tap from a gun with a different sound reached Pete's ears, and he knew that he had been saved.

Rich ran a lung-bursting sprint through the ancient woodland thick with gnarled tree roots. He had almost a quarter of a mile to cover on bad ground. In his day, he would have covered that in less than three minutes.

He ran, slipping twice and scrabbling to his feet to continue as he counted more shots from ahead and to his right. He was blowing hard, but he knew there had to be more in the tank. He paused, finding where Pete had stopped the vehicles by killing two drivers. The cars were abandoned, the occupants gone forward on foot. The foliage was too thick to see into the distance, but the steady rhythm of gunshots still came, only now it was mixed with the staccato sound of return fire from something smaller firing automatic bursts. He turned to his left again and ran as hard as he could for two hundred metres to gain the high ground. He steadied his breath, checked his weapon and crept down towards the road, scanning.

Movement ahead, he raised the gun in a fluid motion and instinctively fired twice into the middle of the body in front of him. He moved forward, willing himself to go on despite his fear.

Movement to his right. Two of them. He dropped one knee and aimed, firing twice more into each shape. He forced himself to his feet to keep moving.

He was lost in himself, a machine designed to kill the enemy quicker than they could kill him. His weapon drills were slick and spoke of long hours of practice he'd feared he had forgotten. He was alive, he was angry, and they would be sorry.

~

"NOW!" Neil screamed.

Jimmy gunned the engine of the small lorry, making it jolt forward to unveil the heavy machine gun mounted in the bed of the truck.

Neil opened up on the lead vehicle, heavy bullets punching through metal and plastic easily. At that distance, it was butchery. The front vehicle swerved off the road into a fence where it stopped dead against a tree, exposing the second car in line to the murderous fire.

Leah took careful aim on the windscreen of the tail-end vehicle. As soon as Neil began to fire, she put four rounds in quick succession straight where the driver's centre mass would be.

The car lost control and slammed into the rear of the second vehicle, which had ground to a halt. Leah scanned along the wreckage, searching for a target. A rear door opened on the last car on the side away from her, and a tentative head popped into view and looked forward to where it thought the danger was.

"Over here," she whispered to herself, like in the film she shouldn't have watched about the alien who killed all the soldiers in the jungle.

She fired, immediately searching for a new target.

Neil fired only occasional bursts now while she scanned for movement.

They were hiding in the dead ground on the other side of the vehicles. Rich would have been there, but he had gone to ambush the ones attacking Pete. She waited for a break in the firing and bawled Neil's name as loudly as she could.

"What?" he shouted back.

"Fire under two," she shouted. They had to be forced from cover before they had a chance to reorganise and fire back.

"What?" he yelled again.

"FIRE. UNDER. THE. SECOND. CAR!" she screamed, carefully pronouncing each word.

They heard her and started to move.

Neil sent three bursts under the car, splaying two of the attackers out on the ground and making another two run for the nearest cover of the treeline.

She lined up on the first one, judged his speed, and fired just in front of him. She fired a second and third bullet into him as he hit the ground.

The other one was gone.

Joe had thrown himself into the bushes to cut the corner between the farm and the road. He now lay flat, catching his breath.

He heard the undergrowth being trampled, and the sound was fast approaching him. He knelt up, rifle scanning the bushes ahead. Too big to be a dog – not even Ash – and no farm animals were anywhere near this woodland. The noise was coming fast, desperate sounds escaping the runner as they blindly fled the heavy firing coming from the house.

Then movement to his right. He turned instinctively and fired a short burst. He was rewarded with the thump of a person hitting the ground.

Dan nearly had his heavy vehicle on two wheels as he drove as hard as he could. He tore down the driveway with Steve bouncing off the window as he swapped his rifle for the carbine.

He slowed to a stop when he saw a wrecked convoy spoiling the views of their home. He got out, and he and Steve went along each side of the vehicles in tandem. Six dead. He ran the last three hundred metres to the house, forgetting about his Land Rover and the dog guarding it. Neil met him there, shouting for Rich, who was nowhere to be found.

Leah had climbed down from her perch and was running over.

"He heard Pete open up and ran back through the woods to help," she shouted over them.

Neil and Dan glanced at each other. Dan suddenly realised he needed his car and his dog and turned to see Steve driving it towards him, pressed up to the driver's window to be as far away from Ash as he could get. As Steve pulled up, Dan saw Ash was "smiling" at him to show off his teeth.

Dan wasn't in the mood for a possessive dog and shouted at him to leave Steve be. He threw himself behind the wheel and Leah jumped in the back with a reproved Ash. He drove as fast as he could again, cutting out the road and using the grass as the direct route to the track behind their home. He stopped behind a large tree stump which had been Pete's chosen firing position.

Pete had been hit.

Dan yelled at Steve to deal with him, pointing Leah to the high ground on his left as he stalked forward with his weapon up and his dog at his heel.

A low, short whistle sounded to his right. He turned to see Rich, covered in leaf mould and with mud on his face, kneeling in the bushes with his gun up and scanning.

Dan crouched by his side. "Report," he said in a low voice.

"Vehicle ambush, driver killed. Second vehicle tried to go round; driver also killed. Rest went on foot. I hit them from the bushes to the side. Took out four. All dead. Pete killed four including the drivers," Rich said bluntly, giving each succinct sentence like it was a bullet point. It sounded professional.

"Any outstanding?" Dan asked.

"Unsure. Vehicles empty when I saw," he said back, still sweeping the rifle side to side.

"With me, then. Friendlies to the rear and left flank, and don't shoot my fucking dog."

Rich smiled out of the corner of his mouth. It was a grim smile, but it told Dan that the Marine was still connected to the real world, no matter how unreal it had just become.

The three of them stalked forward. Dan and Ash moved, then covered Rich as he leapfrogged. The scene of the ambush Rich pulled on them was gruesome. Four bodies lay quite close to each other, all with neatly grouped pairs of bullet holes in their chests. Dan reckoned that Rich must have fallen on these unsuspecting bastards like a fury.

They got to the vehicles and found nobody alive.

"Find 'em!" he said to Ash, pointing him ahead. If any stragglers had got away, they wouldn't be going far. Ash put his nose to the ground and sniffed around, twice being sent ahead to cast for a scent. Nothing.

They turned and jogged back to Pete's position as Dan called out to Leah not to shoot them. She brought James back with her. He was dazed, but it seemed that something had snapped inside him when he heard Pete cry out.

He poured shotgun rounds towards the sounds of enemy gunfire as fast as he could, making them pause. Rich descended on them immediately afterwards, after they closed up to discuss what to do.

Pete didn't seem badly hurt, but he had a pair of bullets in the fleshy part of his shoulder where it met the upper arm. Leah pulled a clotting field dressing from her vest and replaced the slightly less effective hand of Steve's. She wound it tight, telling Pete to keep pressing on it.

"Get him in the truck; I'll take him to Kate," Dan said. He wanted to leave a guard down there and didn't want it to be the terribly damaged Royal Marine or his teenage protégée.

"Steve, can you hold down here for a while?" he asked. Steve retrieved his big rifle and nodded. Pete was lifted into the back seat, relegating the dog to the boot, much to his annoyance.

"I'll bleed on your seats, lad. I can walk," Pete moaned typically as one of the "don't want to cause a fuss" generation.

"It's leather. It'll wipe clean," Dan replied.

He looked behind him in the mirror as he drove the short distance. He saw an old alcoholic poacher having gunshot wounds treated by a heavily armed teenage girl as a concerned dog with a blood-soaked muzzle licked Pete's sweating head and whimpered in sympathy.

Pete was receiving so much attention he could barely open one of his hip flasks.

Dan glanced to his side where Rich had opened the passenger window to rest his rifle out. Rich was half-turned, as if expecting a contact at any moment.

"Rich," Dan said, "tell me where you are."

Without taking his eyes off the landscape, he replied, "Not Afghanistan. Or Iraq or Belfast. But right now just as bloody dangerous. I'm good, boss, seriously." He knew exactly what Dan meant.

They pulled up at the front of the house and Dan yelled for Kate. Pete was making a huge racket, telling everyone he was fine and that he could walk. He tried but ended up more carried upright than walking.

He took his dignity intact into medical, although that dignity was still holding a hip flask as though his life depended on it. As Kate walked out, Leah gave her a casualty-style history just as she had taught her.

"Male, sixties, GSW times two, upper right arm and shoulder. No exit wound. Field dressing with coagulant applied less than five ago."

Kate thanked her, as though receiving a verbal trauma report from a teenager with a machine gun was perfectly normal.

"I'm fifty-eight, you little shit!" yelled Pete half in jest as he was led away inside.

WHAT THE HELL JUST HAPPENED?

Dan called everyone together. He told Jimmy and Neil what he wanted and left them to it. He warned them to be careful, as Steve, Lexi and Joe were still deployed. He told Leah she was with him, and asked Rich to get on the radio and tell the gardens he was on his way back and that they had repelled an attack on the house.

"Tell them I'm coming to talk to Ash's chew toy," he added nastily.

Rich knew he was being benched now that the state of emergency was over, and he took it gracefully. He felt proud of himself. He felt useful for the first time since his life was changed by a crude roadside firebomb.

Marie burst from the main doors carrying a shotgun and demanding to know what was going on. Dan tried the "not now" tactic and nearly lost his head as she bit it off.

"Tell me what happened!" she said, somewhat close to his face and showing a dangerous look in her eyes: a mixture of fear and rage.

"The gardens were attacked by three people with sawn-offs. Steve killed one, Cedric another, and Ash ripped the last one half to pieces. He's still alive for now, but I will be having a chat with him very soon."

She absorbed this quickly, knowing that she would get the full details from everyone in turn. "And?" she said.

"And it was a diversion. They were coming here, which they did in two convoys, front and rear. Pete stopped the rear convoy but took a couple in the shoulder. James fired at them enough to confuse them into bunching up, then Rich hit them from the side. You can see what happened there," he said, indicating the smoking ruins of three Swiss-cheese-like vehicles in the near distance behind him.

There was so much to take in that she said nothing for now. She simply raised herself on her tiptoes and kissed him gently. She handed him the shotgun like it was making her hands dirty and told him to come back safe.

He turned away and tossed the shotgun to Rich before getting back behind the wheel and driving up the road, only to stop by the driveway entrance where Joe was dragging a body from the trees.

Dan stopped and looked at the man. He was filthy, with long hair and a matted beard. He stank. He looked such a mess that Joe had to point out that it was Kyle. Dan stared in silence for a while at the emaciated body of the man who had tried to kill him once.

"Well done, Joe," he said. "Take him down to the others. We'll be back soon."

They reached the gardens and Dan asked where the prisoner was. He was not doing well, but he didn't have to last long for what Dan wanted.

"Oi, fuckface. Remember me?" Dan said as he slapped the prisoner back into consciousness, looking at the butcher's mess of his arm and noticing that two fingers were badly dislocated and splayed out at grotesque angles.

If Leah was affected by the sight of a badly wounded man being mistreated, she showed no sign of it. Dan doubted if she knew about either the Geneva Convention or the Human Rights Act.

Pain racked his face as the consciousness brought back the feeling of the mangled flesh that used to be his forearm.

"Of course you do. Now, I've got a job for you. If you do it properly, I'll get you medical care. If you don't, I'll feed you to my dog." Dan snapped his fingers in front of the guy's face as he was drifting away again.

He nodded.

Dan liked to keep the rules simple. He had his hands tied together at the front and bandaging around the jagged wounds. Leah put her rifle in the front seat out of his reach and sat behind Dan as their prisoner was dumped in where Dan could see him in the mirror behind the passenger's seat. Ash rode up front, watching.

It was less than a minute before the desperate fool made his move.

Instead of opening the door and rolling out for a bid for freedom, which would have resulted in Dan gently stopping and allowing Ash to exit via the window, he went for Leah's knife on her left shoulder. He was quick, turning and reaching out with his left hand, but as quick as the flurry of movement started, it was ended.

Dan looked back to see Leah's left boot pressing into the guy's throat and holding him painfully against the window. She had drawn her sidearm as fast as a lightning strike and held it pointed at his face as she braced her shoulders against her door and arched her back to increase the pressure. He froze, experiencing yet more agony.

She had it covered.

"Nicely done, Nikita. I think our friend can travel the rest of the way like that," Dan said nonchalantly.

"Roger," came the reply, in a funny voice copied from a film he couldn't remember.

SIMPLE INVESTIGATION

The bodies of the attackers had all been laid out on the drive next to the smoking ruins of the convoy.

Eight of them had been brought up by tractor from the rear attack and laid next to the ten from the three vehicles. Kyle was one of them, marked out as different by his filthy clothing and obvious malnutrition.

Leah released her new best friend's throat, recoiling like a mongoose as she slipped from the vehicle while keeping the foresight of her Glock firmly between his eyes.

Dan dragged him out and marched him to the line of bodies.

"Which one's Billy?" Dan demanded.

The shade of pale purple the man had turned during the journey was fading, and he had just about recovered sufficient breath to speak. "Him," he said, indicating a normal-looking man with bullet holes either side of his skull.

"That was me," Leah said aloud, trying not to sound too proud.

Dan glanced casually from the ambush site to the tower she had been perched on during the attack. *Bloody good shot*, he thought to himself as he fought the urge to offer a high five.

"Excellent answer," he said with a false smile. "You progress to round two. Are these all of your friends apart from the two dead bastards we left where you pointed guns at innocent people?"

He started to cry, a pathetic keening noise which cut through Dan's brain painfully.

They were. His entire gang. Billy's crew, all wiped out. He was sure. No matter how much this psychopath threatened him with his child assassin and his evil dog, no matter how much pain he was in, he was the only one left.

"OK. You can go," Dan said, looking around.

Dan saw only Rangers, Jimmy and Neil, and knew that they were shielded from the house by trees.

"Really?" he asked, the revelation stopping his tears instantly.

"Yes. How far is your place? I'll drop you off," Dan said reasonably.

Dumbstruck, the man's mouth opened and closed a few times as he processed what he had just heard. "You know the athletics stadium? Just off the motorway?" he asked, naïve and hopeful.

"Yes," said Dan, drawing the suppressed Walther from his vest and putting one round behind the man's ear at point-blank range.

Nobody spoke as the man's body slumped to the floor with his friends. His legs gave out just like someone had switched off the power supply. A few seconds of silence reigned as they all stared at the additional body on the ground.

"Well, that was frightfully silly of him," declared Neil in his favourite accent, breaking the silence. "Who would pick a fight with a group of armed gentlemen and expect to get away?"

They laughed at Neil's impression as they all accepted their agreed account of how the man died.

"Silly chap. Still, couldn't be helped, eh? Who wants a cup of tea?"

CLEANUP

The bodies were stripped of anything useful, as were the cars. It had been months since they had burned dead people in the tennis court, but they used petrol to light another fire as they had before. The difference being that they had made these people dead intentionally.

Ewan spent the afternoon using the big forklift to drag the five cars to the track that provided access to the rear by the lake. They were dumped in tight formation to block it completely from the road.

Joe offered to move to the gardens for a while until things settled down, taking his vehicle and extra weaponry.

Everyone was brought in for the day to get to grips with what had just happened.

Marie gave the facts to the assembled group. Now that they numbered over seventy, she had to stand at the pulpit in the chapel – or Diverse Multiple Faith Room, as the sign read – to be heard easily.

She gave the brief facts, left out the gory details, and told everyone what was being done about it. "Some of you will remember Kyle, and the others will have heard about him, I'm sure," she said. "It seems that after he fled from here, a group of undesirable people found him and imprisoned him. He must have given them in-depth details about our home, which allowed them to attack us."

Murmurs rippled around the crowd.

"Their attack was repelled." She spoke loudly and confidently. "Their group is no longer a threat to us. Everyone who knew about this is dead." She let that sink in. "Thanks to the quick thinking and bravery of Cedric, Pete, James, Neil and our Rangers, we are still whole." She looked at each person she named as she spoke. "Rangers were expected to fight – it's what they chose to do. When farmers and gardeners and mechanics put their lives on the line, then that needs recognising to reassure them."

The murmur picked up a notch.

"Now, it's true. Pete has been shot in the attack as he and James defended us."

The murmur dropped in happiness a level.

"But expert medical care from Leah at the scene and then Kate, Lizzie and Alice has saved him. He is now resting in medical and needs time to heal, but I'm sure all of our thoughts are with him." Again, she looked at those as she named them, amazing Dan at how she knew where they were in the crowd.

The murmur swayed from concerned to proud and now returned to happy.

"I know this has been difficult and frightening, but until order is established on a wider scale, then we must do as we have done to protect innocent people." She paused, orchestrating the mood of the crowd like a maestro. "We have all been through bad things since it happened, and more bad things may be in store yet, but today we have proven that we are stronger as a group than these people thought. That's why we're here and they're not."

The excitement rose again as Marie went on with her effective propaganda.

Dan didn't know how she managed the strings so well, but she actually got a cheer at the end of the speech.

Dan wanted nothing more than to take the day off, to get back in bed with Marie. To have had breakfast instead of skipping straight to dinner.

However, he had a dog covered in blood, a damaged Marine in need of a serious checkup, a thirteen-year-old who had just killed three people and seemed to think nothing of it, and a friend in the hospital with two big holes where Kate had pulled bullets out of him.

He had Cedric to manage, who had killed someone with a shotgun as he aimed at Dan's own head – something that hadn't even sunk into his own mind yet. He also had over a dozen people frightened by being held hostage, a shortage of ammunition for the machine gun, and an enemy lair to find and destroy.

"Grant me the serenity," Dan said aloud to himself as he walked through the house. He decided to start with the things he could fix easily; that way his to-do list seemed to make progress.

First stop: Pete. Dan found him happily propped up on a hospital bed with a large clean bandage over his shoulder and his arm in a sling. Kate showed Dan the small bullets she had removed, and told him that she had had to give Pete a little "sauce" to aid his recovery. Dan understood and asked for a quiet report on how much he was having to keep functioning.

Pete accepted the thanks blithely, playing down the evident sacrifice he would have most likely made had James not done what he did and Rich not chosen to come to their rescue.

Dan provided Kate with a bottle of Scotch to help her keep Pete happy and save on the medication. He fetched Ash and headed for

Ops, looking for Leah or Rich or both. He found both. All the weapons that had been used that day were stripped fully and put back together oiled. The big machine gun had suffered a jam on the last burst, and Neil had been unable to clear it. The gun now lay in pieces, the delegate components laid out in OCD straight lines on a clean cloth.

Leah and Rich sat at the table looking over the new weapons picked up from their attackers. They were arguing kind-heartedly over which gun had injured Pete.

Rich was adamant that it was the ancient and very illegal Uzi automatic pistol with filed-off serial numbers. That thing had probably changed hands numerous times over the last thirty years as it made its rounds through the criminal underworld, being held sideways and pointed out of car windows.

"Right calibre, two wounds close together. High rate of fire. It was this," Rich said, resting his finger on the dull and uncared-for weapon.

"OK, maybe you're right," Leah admitted.

"You two gun geeks have any other hobbies?" Dan asked them.

"No. Not really," Leah said, deadly serious.

Dan sighed. He knew she would never have the end of her childhood as she deserved, but the fact that she seemed to enjoy it so much concerned him sometimes.

"Fine. I've got a search-and-rescue mission for you instead. Solo. Can you do it?" he asked seriously.

"Yes. Details?" she said, jumping up.

"Ops. Missing bottle of single malt. Not been seen for two days. Should be in company with a glass. Go."

Leah knew when she'd been played, and walked off to fetch what she was sent for. Dan opened one of the large windows and sat on the floor with his head resting on the sill. He lit a cigarette and answered the dog's grumbling with, "Shut it, tobacco Nazi." Ash put his head down with a grumble and didn't press the issue.

Leah returned with the bottle and glass, taking her leave before she was sent. Dan had already primed Marie to intercept her.

"Do your teeth before bed," he called after her.

"Yes, Dad," came the sarcastic reply.

Some dad, he thought.

Both Leah and Rich knew what the shakedown was for, and she knew she would be sent away so Dan could do his "after-action" report. He poured himself a measure and suddenly realised how thoughtless he was being. He started to apologise to Rich, who stopped him.

"It's fine. I can choose to drink or not. Today isn't really a celebration day for me, so I won't be having one. But thanks."

Dan raised his glass to him anyway and took a sip.

"I wanted to ask you something," Dan started.

"I'm fine. I went into a bit of autopilot and I was scared. Really scared, actually," Rich said, fiddling with the extended magazine from the Uzi.

"I was actually going to ask what made you leave the post you were given," Dan said quietly.

Rich stopped fiddling and looked at him coldly.

"That came out wrong," Dan said, backtracking. "What I meant was, how did you know to reinforce the rear?"

Rich calmed down immediately, having momentarily thought he had been accused of desertion because Dan had not been careful with his words.

"Two civvies out back, three trained out front. Judgement call," he said, almost grudgingly.

Dan took a sip of his drink. "You did bloody well. You saved lives, possibly all of ours. I need you to understand that this isn't the military; there's no chain of command with orders to obey, not really. I don't have the monopoly on good ideas, and I appreciate having people around me who can think independently. What matters to me is that you got the job done. You saw a leak and you plugged it. Not only that, you dropped four people who looked like they hadn't even seen you."

"They hadn't," Rich said, smiling wickedly out of the scarred corner of his mouth.

Dan raised the glass to him again. "What about our resident child assassin? Did you hear what she did in the back of my truck?"

He hadn't. Dan filled him in on the details. Rich laughed heartily as he imagined Leah going "full ninja", as he put it.

"I honestly don't know what to make of her sometimes," Rich said. "She doesn't show any signs I'd recognise as anything being wrong. Maybe she's just adapted to it?"

Dan took another drink, draining the glass. "Maybe," he answered. "I just sometimes wish she'd refuse to get out of bed or something. You know, be a normal teenager?"

"You can't expect her to be normal," explained Rich. "We don't live in a normal world anymore."

"True," said Dan. "Anyway, I'm officially bloody impressed with your work. Are you looking to get out and about?" He was offering him a shot at being a Ranger, and Rich surprised him.

"Not yet, no," Rich said. "I've honestly spent enough of my life creeping along waiting to get shot at. I'd like to stay as quartermaster and look at the defences for this place if I can?"

Dan was happy with that. "What about special occasions? Can we dust you off for the odd one?"

He laughed. "Dawn raid, guest starring me?"

"Yeah," said Dan.

Rich nodded his agreement, and offered him his congratulations on a successful day. Dan shook his maimed hand as he left.

Dan looked for Leah and found her walking with Marie to her office, each carrying a hot chocolate from a large batch made up by Nina. Dan went back to Ops and poured himself another drink as Ash whined nervously at Satan's reincarnation. The cat had been dislodged from its normal perch as Rich had sorted out the ammunition properly, so it now chose to lounge on a shelf with its legs hanging down. It avoided the shopping basket bed and preferred the height advantage from which to tease the dogs.

Steve sat reading a book with his feet up by the window, which looked along the drive. The CB set to his right was silent and the coffee to his left looked cold.

The pilot looked up from his book long enough to give a friendly nod. Dan liked that about Steve: he could do comfortable silences.

Dan wandered out to find Cedric and thank him for saving his life. He also planned to ask him if he would kindly not mention to Marie how close he had been to getting his head blown off.

THE LAIR

Dan did not entirely trust Ash's friend that the whole group had come in force to take over their home. He planned to make sure.

Leah and Rich were left as guard, and he took the three Rangers to work in pairs. They went in two vehicles, Dan in his Discovery with Joe and Ash, and Steve behind in his Defender with Lexi.

He knew the stadium, as it was the only one within a fifty-mile radius at least. The main reason they had never come across this group was that there were no real main roads that connected their areas, and to find them would have made for an illogical and ponderous journey. If one of them had panicked and fled blindly across country for over ten miles, they might have found the place eventually.

As they approached, they saw a supermarket on the opposite side of the road. That was why they weren't struggling for supplies or having to go out anywhere. Kyle dropping in must have been something of a surprise for them.

Across the front of the supermarket were the painted words "CLAIMED: LOOTERS WILL BE KILLED". Friendly people.

They had stopped the cars short of the building and made the last half mile on foot, working in two pairs covering and moving in silence.

They found the place abandoned, with evidence of where the occupants had slept and a cache of bags ready to be collected after they had established themselves in their new home. It had been well planned, but by amateurs. They deserved their fate. They had made no attempt to plan for the future, either through inability or a lack of imagination. Did they really expect to survive forever like this?

Lexi emptied all the bags looking for anything useful and found nothing. They had put all their eggs in one basket and had had it knocked from their hands as they deserved.

Dan cleared the upper level with Ash as the others did the same downstairs. Nobody home. Either there were others and they had fled after the rest didn't come home, or Dan had extracted the truth before he shot the only survivor in the head. They returned to the vehicles and poured coffee, deciding what to do with the rest of the day. Steve laid out a road map on the bonnet of the Discovery as Dan wondered aloud if there were any groups of survivors left who weren't arseholes.

Lexi knew the towns of a nearby county, having grown up there. Steve, not being from the area originally, went with Joe in his own Defender towards the countryside in the direction they were pointing. Lexi went with Dan and Ash, as that way, both crews had a sniper option if needed.

They wished each other luck and planned to be back home by nightfall. Dan called up home on the CB and got Rich straight away.

"Go ahead, boss," Rich said.

"Nothing here. Intel must have been good. Splitting into two teams for recce further afield. Back by nightfall," Dan replied.

"Roger. Happy hunting, and stay safe," Rich came back.

The weather was blowing cold and wet as Dan drove along endless fifty-mile-an-hour roads, thinking that the commute along here would have been dull. They reached a small town that didn't even have a full supermarket and saw that the windows had been broken long ago, probably before the winter.

They pressed on, going from small town to village as they went. Each settlement showed aged signs of having been systematically emptied of supplies. They were probably two hours from home when Lexi pointed out a vehicle that didn't look right.

Dan rolled to a stop and killed the engine. They watched from a distance, waiting for anyone to return to the small truck which was obviously still in use; no vehicle which had been left idle for over half a year would be in such good condition. Everywhere, the cars were covered in old dead leaves and a green film of neglect, but this one had fresh windscreen wiper marks showing clear glass.

"Play it nice, or play it careful?" he asked the car out loud. Ash stopped panting to give a small grumble and nuzzle his face. Lexi suggested that they play it nice.

Dan started the car and drove slowly forwards. As they neared the car, he stopped and went to get out. Lexi followed suit.

"No," he said, "wait here. If they aren't friendly, then let Ash out and you follow."

She nodded and let go of her door handle.

Dan slipped out, walking slowly and keeping the barrel of his gun pointing towards the floor. He got his familiar feeling of being watched and hoped it wasn't through the sights of anything which went *bang*. He stopped by the car, looking around.

"Hello?" he called out, and waited. He looked around, fighting the urge to raise the weapon and use the scope for better detail. He knew Lexi would be itching to get out, but they had to give off the vibe of being friendly.

46

"Hello?" he tried again, louder.

A noise behind him made him turn to see a man dressed in camouflage clothing in a doorway. He held a large rifle, the same size as their own battle rifles but this one was older with a wooden stock.

"Hello," he said back, keeping his own gun pointed at the floor.

Dan took his hands away from his weapon to make a point of it. "Friendly," he said. "We've met plenty who weren't, but I'm hoping you are."

The man regarded him closely. He was older than Dan, older than Steve too. He carried himself well and had the look of a professional man at one point before he grew his hair and beard long and wild. He kept the gun where it was. "What about your friend in the car?" he asked.

"She means no harm either. We've taken to travelling in pairs because there has been some trouble. You experienced any?" he asked.

"We've had our share," he said carefully.

We, thought Dan. "How many is we?" he asked, hopeful.

"Not sure I should say just yet. No offence," the man replied.

"There are about seventy of us, mostly farming and growing crops. Only the explorers like me go around dressed like this," Dan said with a smile, hoping to reassure the man that he wasn't from a military camp.

"Seventy?" he asked, straightening slightly. "That's good going." He seemed to consider his situation for a little longer, then relaxed a bit and allowed the gun to rest on its sling, which he put over a shoulder. "Name's Gregory," he said, "you?"

"Dan," he said, pointing his thumb at himself before turning over to his left side. "Lexi's in the car with my dog."

"Truce?" Gregory suggested.

"We mean no harm; I swear it," Dan replied.

Gregory walked from the building and came out, still keeping clear of this armed and armoured man who had walked into his world.

"Shall we talk?" asked Dan.

"Not here. Follow me," replied Gregory, climbing into his car.

NEIGHBOURS

They followed Gregory away from the main road onto a playing field. It was overgrown but well-trodden in places where Gregory had driven in before. He turned his car around to face them and stopped.

Gregory emerged slowly, the rifle held low in one hand. Dan unclipped the carbine and left it on his seat, and he walked towards the man carrying only his suppressed Walther and the brute of a shotgun on his back. Lexi emerged similarly disarmed but with a sidearm visible in the holster on her chest.

Dan brought one extra item with him: his flask of coffee, which he raised to Gregory as they neared.

He nodded. "I've got biscuits," he said without a hint of humour.

After a bit of standoffish acceptance, they finally relaxed in each other's company sufficiently to talk.

"I found some folks about a week after. I'd loaded up all my stuff to go and find out what was happening but realised it was everywhere and I wouldn't know where to start. They already live a bit like this, you know, all environmental and that," he explained. "I don't stay there all the time when the weather's good. I drive around looking for people and things."

Dan reciprocated with their own story, leaving out some details such as raiding other camps and killing everyone or having their own home attacked and killing all of them, too. He worried it might give the wrong impression of them. *The words "I can explain" never really help*, he thought.

"We managed to get holed up well before winter, and now we have a farm and a commercial garden with greenhouses." Dan went on to say about their solar power and hot water, which made Gregory's eyes open wider.

"Will you take us to your group?" Lexi asked.

Gregory swallowed his drink as he thought. "Follow me. It'll take about twenty minutes."

They all talked as they drove, running through options. Could they recruit these survivors to come back with them? Would they want to? How did they generate power? Fresh water?

They followed Gregory down a farm track and saw curious-looking buildings. There were signs by the entrance making bold statements about geothermal heating and emission-free homes. They had found some kind of hippy camp, Dan thought, and he tried to practise his nonjudgemental face.

He would be fine as long as they didn't try to get him to meditate with them or give him an earth name or something else ridiculous.

As it was, their minds were blown by the peace of the place. They were well situated in a valley with low, rolling hills either side. They had a well and were in the process of building a timber-framed house with straw walls. They explained how they would put timber boards over the frame and pack the whole thing with mud and other things to make it weather-tight. Everyone seemed happy and smiled at them as they walked around, feeling totally alien with their black clothes and guns. It was like these people had come from a different world and not the same violent dystopia that his own group had escaped.

They had a small working farm, complete with another well, and when Dan talked about the breeding problems on their own farm, someone mentioned that they had a bull, and two cockerels which had to be permanently separated to stop them from killing each other.

As they toured the place, the word *commune* sprang to Dan's head. He had thoughts emerging that they could trade with these people if they had things that each other wanted.

They were invited into the main building, which was formerly the visitors' centre, where a person could pay just under five pounds for a homemade tea bag made up of wild berries and other spices or over six for a small bottle of pear and elderflower cider. They probably both tasted like toilet water, Dan decided, vowing to stick to coffee and Scotch.

They sat, and the apparent leader of the group sat down to speak with them. She was a thin old woman, permanently smiling in a serene manner. Dan would have probably found her very annoying a year ago, but then he wouldn't have been sitting here dressed as he was a year ago.

They were offered refreshments, and both Lexi and Dan chose water.

"My name is Scarlet," she said, and they introduced themselves to her in turn. She didn't look like a Scarlet; she was at least sixty and had white hair which hung thinly to her shoulders.

"As you have seen, we have been blessed here," she said. It turned out that most of the people here had come in the first week. They were either workers or regular visitors to the site, and they all agreed that their little corner of peace was the best place to rebuild.

"We have saved over forty people from the harshness of the outside," she said mystically, "and we are nearly all of us happy here."

Interesting, he thought. "Nearly?" he asked.

"Some of those brought here do not like our way of life. They long for the things they have lost, you see?" she explained. The slow way she spoke was starting to get on his nerves. "We have two of the younger ones who express a wish to leave, but they have not because it is not safe," she finished.

"What about Gregory? Why don't they go with him?" Lexi asked.

"Gregory is happy in his own company and will not take them with him. He visits occasionally, bringing those he finds in need of help, but his wish is to live alone."

In the current company, Dan thought he could understand why. He got to the point. "The way I see it, we can be of use to each other. We can swap the stud animals for the farm to ensure the breeds live on. We grow our own vegetables and will be adding salads to the list as soon as the weather gets better. I'm offering to establish trade," he said.

Scarlet smiled sickeningly. "I think that is wise. Will you return here one week from today? If you speak to Zachary, I'm sure he can help."

Dan thanked her and stood to leave.

"If you don't mind, I have another request," Scarlet said.

"Go on," he replied.

"The younger ones we have who do not like it here. They do not share our philosophies and our beliefs; will you speak with them? Explain the dangers of the outside world?"

Dan said he would, but he had his own suggestion. "And if they still want to see the world? What then?"

"What are you suggesting?" Scarlet asked, the curtain of tranquillity over her face twitching to betray her thoughts.

"If they want to go, they can come with us. If they want to come back, we will bring them back when we return. You have my word," he said firmly.

Scarlet smiled again, glad that she had manoeuvred this man to where she wanted him. In truth, she couldn't stand those kids: they were loud and they didn't respect nature. They wanted to eat the cows and the chickens instead of nurturing them for their eggs and milk.

"Very well," she said magnanimously.

They went outside to find Zachary. He was every bit the vegetarian organic farmer Dan expected, and he doubted that anything the man wore had ever had a label in. They discussed livestock, Dan's knowledge being just about sufficient to do the trade, and he agreed to bring back the bull and cockerel for straight swaps as well as a few of last year's lambs to swap for one of their own yearling rams. *This should allow the livestock population to enlarge a bit quicker*, he thought, then went to find the ones who didn't fit in.

VEGETARIAN PRISON

Henry was maybe a little older than Leah, and very easily bored. He had even taken to doing press-ups obsessively in an attempt to impress the older girls from the group. There were two of them, and he took their giggling to mean that he was getting somewhere when in fact they were laughing at him.

Lucy was ten and looked as though she had just given up. She looked at the chicken pen for hours, longing for the chance to cook one of the ungainly birds and eat every last scrap of flesh from its bones. It consumed her; she dreamed of roast chicken.

Neither enjoyed it there, and both had a similar story in that they were found and brought here, one by Gregory and one by a kind woman who harboured thoughts of raising her for future breeding.

They both rebelled: both were punished by being sent to sit in solitary boredom for hours at a time. Neither of them wanted to work, and neither wanted to stay.

"Have you tried to leave?" Dan asked them.

Henry did once, but he came back. He wouldn't admit that he was scared, and Dan doubted if he'd even got to the main road. Lucy hadn't; she just sat bored. They were both unhappy.

Lexi began to tell them about their home. As she spoke, the kids looked up. They grew more attentive with each line she spoke, and when finally they were offered to come and live with them instead, both jumped up to say yes. They would both have probably asked anyway. Dan couldn't believe how trusting these people were, or maybe he underestimated just how much they didn't like people who didn't fit in. He recognised it for what it was: it was one bizarre meeting about the power of Mother Nature away from being a cult.

Dan had no great wish to involve the spiritual in their lives – a person's beliefs were their own, he thought. He very much believed in the concept of each to their own, but having to live under the stifling blanket of a faith you didn't want would be too much to cope with. Both kids packed their small amount of belongings and barely held their excitement as they bounced to the Discovery.

Dan turned to Scarlet, seeing her flanked by younger women dressed in the same way as her.

"We will be back to trade in a week; if the kids don't like it there, they will be brought back then."

Scarlet nodded sagely.

He noticed that not one person said goodbye to the children. He turned and unlocked the Land Rover, asking them to wait. "Ash, over," he said, making the reluctant dog jump into the boot.

Lucy made a noise at seeing him, and Dan explained to them both.

"He is not a pet. Please don't put your hands through to him or he might bite you." He struggled for the words to get it through to them exactly what Ash was.

Lexi stepped in. "Did either of you ever see a police dog?" she asked. Both nodded. "Well, until Ash knows you and gets used to you, just be careful of him, OK? Don't try and stroke him!"

They understood.

Henry's face when he saw their guns was a picture; his eyes grew so wide on seeing the shotgun that he could barely speak or break his gaze away.

Dan talked as he drove. "There are a few of us who make sure that everyone is safe. We're the ones who go out and make the dangerous places less dangerous. It's not for everyone, but it needs to be done so we can live in safety. We're called Rangers."

Henry showed his immaturity by asking outright if he could be one too.

"It's about what training we've had," Dan said, thinking that he had to come up with an excuse for a girl younger than him having weapons. "We all have previous experience, which takes years to learn. You'll have to see how it goes, get really fit, and try when you're older. If you want to stay, that is."

Henry sank back in his seat. Lucy said nothing for about thirty miles, until she asked, "What's for lunch?"

They had left "The Haven," as they had called it, before mealtime, and Dan looked to Lexi. She dug into her E&E bag and came out with snack bars, crisps, and two bottles of water.

"Here," she said, handing them back and ignoring Ash's best "I'm a good boy" face with his top lip tucked behind a row of teeth. "We usually eat lunch on the go as we work. There'll be a hot meal tonight, though."

Neither kids really heard her; they were ripping into the carbo-hydrate-rich food like they had spent years in a Turkish prison, their faces melting with the satisfaction of the taste of food they weren't allowed.

A few questions came from the back as they drove, and the four spoke about the way life went in their own personal manor house. Ash watched Lexi for a while, still waiting for his treat. He gave up, grumbled, and turned to look out of the rear window.

GAINS AND LOSSES

They arrived back before Steve and Joe, sedately coming down the drive and rolling over the patches on the tarmac where the blood and fluids from the wrecked cars were starting to wash away.

Both made the right noises as the ornate building came into sight, although Dan felt that its original grandeur was slightly marred by the solar panels which looked like they had landed from space on the roof.

Dan pulled up to his usual space by the front door and climbed out.

"Hang on here for a minute with them," he said to Lexi. She nodded. Dan let Ash out of the boot and nearly tripped over him as he made straight for the nearest tyre to irrigate it. Leah met him at the door. She was wearing a belt holster with an identical gun to Dan's new Walther, which was sitting proudly on her skinny left hip in a cross draw position.

He smiled at her and asked for Marie and Kate to come and meet the newbies. Leah tiptoed and strained her eyes past him but couldn't see inside the Discovery's tinted windows.

Kate was the first out, asking Dan who he had found.

"Hang on for a minute. I'll explain in one go. Is Lizzie free to give them a tour while we talk?"

She nodded and went inside, bringing Alice and Lizzie out for induction duties.

Marie appeared, having politely cut short one of her sessions with a survivor from the shipping container cage. Rich stayed in Ops; he didn't like the stares his scars got from people who didn't know him.

Dan beckoned Lexi to bring them out and a smiling but nervous ten-year-old Lucy and fourteen-year-old Henry were introduced. Henry's eyes rested on Leah's left hip, but a respectable attempt at a death stare from her made him look away embarrassed. Dan reminded himself to explain to Henry that Leah wasn't on the menu, not unless he wanted an injury or three.

Lizzie and Alice took them in for the tour and for new clothes, as they were still in the white linen outfits of the "organic fanatics", as Lexi had named them.

As they went inside out of sight, Dan leaned back against his vehicle and lit a smoke. Lexi and Marie did the same, and he wondered that it was strange how the idea to light a cigarette was socially catching. Rich walked out to hear the debrief and stood behind Leah.

Dan explained about meeting the slightly weird loner guy, and how he led them to The Haven. The way he explained the place actually made it sound really good, so he shot their collective hopes down by making a point of it seeming like a cult.

"Lexi calls them the organic fanatics," he said.

Lexi shrugged. "It's accurate," she added.

"Anyway, it seems to us that they have no interest in having these kids back, so unless they have a big change of heart, they are ours now."

Nobody disagreed with Dan's statement.

Marie went back inside to make plans for the children to be inducted properly and found living space. Not only that, they needed a chaperone as such to start with. Kate followed, readying for another two medical histories to be taken. Dan saw Lexi look at her watch. He knew Paul would be in the gym now, and he was feeling generous.

"I'll go speak to Chris about the trade; take the afternoon off," he said. She lit up and walked inside to secure her kit, thanking him.

Dan called her back to take his carbine and shotgun. He walked up to the farm with Ash sniffing along the hedgerows beside him. He found Chris talking with Melissa and gave them both the rundown on the hippy farm.

Chris was annoyed. "How could I have forgotten that place?!" he cursed himself. He went on to say how they used pre-machinery farming methods and described the place as the closest the area had to an Amish community. They thought the gene pool swap was a great idea, and Chris asked to accompany him on the return trip.

"Of course you can," Dan agreed. "You think I'm taking a bull anywhere without your help?"

Plans were made, and Melissa turned to Chris to give him her new ideas for expansion. The timing of it would allow them to get lambs out of this coming season. He bid his farewells, leaving the Farm Manager and Chief Geneticist to their discussions, and walked back to the house as he smoked. The realisation of a Penny legacy put a smile on his face, as he had unwittingly given his friends grand titles.

He got back and was immediately collared by Leah to come and see what they had done. The large map covering one wall had been moved, as they had been sorting out the office now it wasn't partly an ammo store. In doing so, they had uncovered a large blackboard which must have become defunct when the prison had years ago turned to computers to manage their roll call. It had a grid system for writing in numbers of prisoners based on where they were. There was a section for the farms, the gardens, the works party, the kitchens, and others. Leah and Rich had scrubbed off some sections and added new ones using Tippex. The "total count" section at the bottom right became their first official population counter.

"Now, when someone goes out," said Leah excitedly, "we mark down how many go to what place and mark them back in." She made a point of rubbing R1 and R2 off of the section "Ranging" and adding two to the count in the house. He looked at her: seeing a young girl so pleased with herself for doing something new made his heart melt a little. He really was pleased with her and proud of her work. His eyes rested on the Walther on her hip, and he was about to say something about her using a weapon she hadn't been trained with. He decided not to; this girl had done everything and more to get his approval and to be the best she could be at everything she did. She had killed to protect her home, and he thought that he should probably give her some leeway. It was way past the point where he didn't trust her with weapons, so he let it slide.

"Good work. I'm impressed!" he said. "You two sure you can keep on top of this, then? Lots of people moving in and out nowadays."

"We've got it under control, boss," said Rich, giving a conspiratorial wink behind Leah's back. Dan turned to her.

"I see you've switched to the P99 too?" he said.

She placed her left hand on the weapon, slightly self-consciously. "Yeah, I like the weight of it. It feels chunky," she said quietly, not wishing to sound childish by admitting that she wanted to carry the same gun as him.

"Me too," he said, satisfied with the flattery of imitation.

He walked to the dining room to get a hot coffee.

The kids were excited about the place, not giving any indication that they thought it was a temporary arrangement. He was happy with that. Word went around those in the house quickly about the new arrivals, and he found a small huddle around them. He saw Lucy tucking into a plate of jam tarts brought out by Cara, who was ever happy to see people enjoying her treats. Henry was telling them about the place where they had been, and he wasn't making it sound very welcoming. Dan noticed Eve listening intently, lapping up every word he said.

He hadn't thought of her for a while – her or the child who spent months attached to her leg. He couldn't see the girl now and looked around for her. He leaned closer to Nina as she walked past carrying drinks for the kids and asked her where she was.

"She's moved into Cara's room now," she said, shocked that Dan didn't know. "Both the little ones stay with her, but the girl still doesn't talk to anyone."

He felt a little bit bad for not knowing, but then reasoned with himself that he wasn't exactly idle and couldn't be expected to know the social ins and outs of over seventy people. He left them to it and went to find something constructive to do.

Carrying his coffee and two jam tarts, he walked out through the lounge area where Ash had curled up on one of the large settees.

Smelling food, Ash jumped down and followed expectantly, receiving the pastry crusts to reinforce his faith in scrounging from people. They walked outside, where Dan lit another cigarette and stood in the cold sunlight.

He suddenly felt very lonely, as if everyone else but him was busy right now. He thought of things he could do to be constructive and settled on a visit to Pete to see how he was healing.

Dan found Pete sitting up in bed with Alice reading to him. He could read just fine, but he liked the company. Not wanting to intrude, Dan nodded his hellos to the pair and left.

Still lost for something to do, he went to his room and took off his boots. With Ash taking up a large portion of the floor – Marie made it clear she was not sharing the bed with him too – he lay back and picked up the book he had on the table next to the bed. He'd meant to start reading it about six months ago, but until now he hadn't had the chance.

He must have dozed off at one point, because Marie woke them both, having looked everywhere for him to say dinner was ready. As they walked downstairs, she said that Eve had come to talk to her. She beat around the bush a lot, but she wanted to go on the trade run to see The Haven. Dan saw no real reason to refuse her, so agreed.

ESTABLISHING TRADE

The week went quickly, and on the day their first trade caravan went out, Dan met an excited Chris ready with a Land Rover and the horsebox trailer. He towed the bull with a lividly aggressive chicken sitting in a cage on the back seat. Ana was driving a pickup not dissimilar to Thunderbird Two, only hers had a tin cover on and half a dozen sheep in the back instead of a huge machine gun.

Dan left Ash with Leah, which caused him more worry than giving her guns did. He was satisfied that they would be fine, as Ash would just spend the day in Ops waiting for her to feed him.

They wove their way through the towns and villages until Dan recognised a familiar vehicle sitting on an approach to the road. He pointed it out to Eve, who had remained annoyingly silent the whole journey. As he slowed down near Gregory's car, allowing him to pull out and lead the way, Eve sat up.

"I've seen that car before," she said. Dan looked at her. "Just before you turned up, that was the car I saw the soldier in."

Dan thought for a minute. If she had stepped out and spoken to Gregory instead of hiding, then she and the girl would have probably been brought here months ago and saved him from hearing her whine.

They pulled up after bouncing along the track, and Eve's eyes lit up. She got out of the car and walked slowly as if in a daze. Dan got out and waved the others through to the farm area, hoping to get done quickly. Zachary shook hands with Chris and, maybe Dan imagined it, flinched from the strength of his grip. They spoke briefly, then organised the loading and unloading of animals.

Dan walked to the visitors' centre or whatever they called it now to find Eve sitting with Scarlet and her two flanking clones. They were drinking some kind of herbal infusion, which boring people like him would probably call tea.

He had never seen Eve smile, and she was smiling now. He was invited to sit down and a cup of infused something or other was poured for him. He tried it, and found it to taste like shit. He politely swallowed and put the cup down, resisting the urge to spit it out.

"Well, ask him, child," urged Scarlet with a false smile of serenity.

Eve straightened herself in her carved wooden seat, then looked at him. "I want to stay," she said with a grand amount of drama.

"OK," he said, and then turned to Scarlet. "They're swapping animals now. Shall we make this a yearly thing to keep our herds healthy?"

Scarlet seemed taken back that he hadn't made more of an issue about Eve's big news. "Yes, that seems like a wonderful idea," she said, recovering her poise.

Eve tried again to get a reaction. "I won't need any of my things. Everything I could want will be provided here," she said.

Except shampoo, conditioner, razors, toothpaste… thought Dan.

"That's fine," he said, not bothering to be as false as the hippies and make up rubbish about how she would be missed and blah, blah,

blah. Truth was, she constantly moaned, wouldn't lift a finger to help, and instead of looking after the traumatised girl who clung to her, she tried to dump her off on anyone else. She had finally succeeded, and if she wanted to go and live in a tepee or whatever and dance in the mud with no shoes on, then that was fine by him.

Dan got up to leave. "Thanks again for your hospitality," he said to Scarlet, receiving an annoying slow nod like she was the oracle of all things. If he didn't like her much before, then he certainly wasn't under her spell now.

He walked to the door and said over his shoulder, "In case you were wondering, the kids wanted to stay with us." He left without waiting for an answer.

He found Chris had loaded the bull without issue but the cockerel he had in exchange was even more foul-tempered than the one they had brought. It was a similar story with the young ram. Its little horns had just started to grow and looked out of place, like a teenage boy with a light fluff of a moustache. He displayed a bit of attitude to Ana until Chris picked it up bodily and slid it into the back of the pickup.

"Good to go," Chris said to Dan with a satisfied smile.

"Me too," Dan replied, smiling wider. "I've done my own trade."

They looked puzzled, until he couldn't contain it any longer. "I've swapped Eve for the kids!"

They were still confused, and he explained that Eve had made a huge drama about announcing that she wanted to stay and be at one with nature. They both laughed with him and began the journey home.

So was established Dan's settlement's first official trade route.

FISH OUT OF WATER

Emma gave up on the idea of using a vehicle after a week. She eventually found a working car on the third day of her journey, living off the remaining food and water she found in abandoned shops still hosting the desiccated remains of the former owners.

The problem was the roads: they were blocked in most places. She hadn't driven in nearly seven years since she had first learned, having lived in university accommodation and used public transport ever since. She didn't know the city from the road perspective, and using trains was clearly no longer an option.

In the end, she had to travel over thirty miles to the south to escape the built-up areas before she began to look for transport again. She travelled lightly, with only the small rucksack containing a few items. She kept the handgun and spare things of bullets – magazines, she believed they were called – and kept the precious laptop safe.

Three times she had to hide when she heard the sounds of other people; she couldn't afford the delay or the inherent risk of interacting with them.

She had taken to travelling on foot during darkness, a darkness so complete as she had never seen before. The lack of light pollution made her see the skies over the city as she never had.

Eventually she found a working vehicle, having used the hill it was parked on to get the engine going.

She began her long, looping journey around the country to find her way north. She had never driven on a motorway before, and found that she had to go slowly and weave between abandoned and crashed cars, their drivers' skeletal remains left where they were exposed.

After she had escaped the city limits, she took to travelling during the daylight, twice in the first day having to go back up the motorway to find an alternative route, as the pileups had blocked the lanes entirely. She made slow progress, made worse on the fourth day of driving when she struggled to siphon enough fuel to keep going. She tried the radio as she drove, finding nothing but static on every station. Not even an emergency broadcast remained, and she wondered if the system had ever even been activated.

She crept northwards, sticking to the centre of the country and using the blue road signs to direct her.

NEW LIFE, OLD LIFE

On Dan's instruction, the Rangers had been hunting in pairs further afield. The farms were a hive of activity, with crops being planted and animals being bred. Chris was happy and excited, claiming that the herds would be doubled within a couple of years. There was fresh meat, and fresh vegetables were starting to ripen. Apple and plum trees were sprouting, and every square inch of greenhouse space at the gardens was either already planted or earmarked for planting soon.

Dan was sleeping off a night shift spent awake in Ops when he woke around lunchtime to noise downstairs: more than normal noise, there was some excitement going on. He dressed in trousers and boots with a T-shirt, fitting a gun behind his back as habitually as lacing his boots. He made his lazy way into the dining room, thinking caffeine thoughts.

A woman and two men were sitting at the tables surrounded by those not out at work. Three new pairs of hands were a good thing, Dan thought as he poured a coffee. He turned and rested against the long table as he sipped. Heads moved in the small crowd and he saw the profile of one of the men.

A flash of recognition hit Dan, making him feel sick to his stomach. He knew this man from his distant past.

He put down his coffee cup without taking his eyes away and reassured himself that the gun was just behind his right hip before he drew himself up to his full height.

"Kelvin Parkes," Dan announced in an icy tone that cut through the noise like a razor.

The room was instantly silenced. One of the inexplicable customs of their new world was that nobody ever used a surname. The man went pale and turned towards him.

"Me? That's not my name!" he said, adding a disarming smile.

The reply gave Dan all the confirmation he needed: that wheedling voice, the slight lisp, the utterly obsequious tone.

It was him, and he absolutely had to go.

"Stand up," Dan commanded.

Others started to speak, to question what he was doing. Some of them had heard that tone of voice before. Andrew watched in confused fear: the last time he'd heard Dan speak like this, he had nearly killed a man in a supermarket with his bare hands.

The man didn't move. He looked around smiling at the other faces in the room in silent appeal for help.

Dan took a step forward and drew himself up.

"Stand up. Now," he said, fighting to contain his rising anger.

"What are you doing?" Marie hissed at him.

He didn't take his eyes off the man and replied, "I'll tell you in a minute."

He stepped forward, now within reach of the sitting man. "Get. Up," he growled.

The man stood, panic evident on his face, and started to speak. Dan's temper finally snapped. He grabbed the man by his jacket and dragged him from the room on his tiptoes, prompting shouts and screams from others.

As Dan dragged the man out of the room, he threw himself on the floor, holding up his hands to fend off Dan's aggression.

Dan dragged him to his feet again, locking his arm behind his back with his left and using his right hand to pull the opposite shoulder. The man moved in pain, arching his back to try and relieve the agonising pressure on his right arm and shoulder.

He pleaded with Dan as he was marched into Ops. Rich looked up in surprise as the disruption burst into his peace.

Dan threw the man into the room, making him stagger to remain standing.

"Rich, search him and don't let him out of your sight," Dan said, snarling.

Rich did as he was asked.

Dan turned to see Marie standing in front of him, furious, and a small crowd gathering behind her.

"What the hell–" she began, lost for words at his sudden violence.

Dan had no choice but to admit what he knew, exposing his own history in doing so. "Because he's a fucking sex offender," he said loudly, silencing them all. "I know this. He was sentenced to ten years in prison."

The mixture of shock and disgust at the revelation left them stunned.

"He will not stay here. I will not allow it," he finished.

He saw Cara at the back of the crowd, ushering the growing gaggle of children away into the house.

"You're sure?" Marie asked quietly.

"Positive. Hand on Bible," he replied. She knew what that meant.

She thought for a moment before asking Rich to watch the man. She nodded her head back inside to indicate that Dan should follow. She walked towards the dining room, sending runners to collect the other council members.

A tense wait ensued while the others were gathered, and Marie sent everyone else from the room.

When they were gathered, Dan asked for a rundown of how the three came to be there.

"Lexi and Joe found them travelling south, told them about this place and brought them here. As we have before," she added, warning Dan not to lay blame.

"Where were they coming from?" he asked. Nobody knew. He suggested bringing the other man in.

He was called Rob. He and the woman had been travelling south to escape the next harsh winter. They found the other man alone, coming from the northeast.

"What story did he give you?" Marie asked.

"Not much, really," said Rob. "He said he'd spent a few years up there working but had no family around. He asked to come with us."

Rob was thanked and invited to leave.

"You all have my word that this man is a dangerous, predatory paedophile," Dan said.

Nobody answered.

"How do you know, mate?" asked Neil quietly.

Dan sagged. "Twelve years ago, I worked not far from here. I was a police officer. A young girl went missing, and by the time we got into her laptop at home, it was too late. He pretended to be her age and arranged to meet her. She got in his car and he took her and repeatedly raped her. We threw everything we had at it and found his car on CCTV picking her up. I found him and locked him up. He still had her blood on his trousers," he said, swallowing hard at the images flashing in his mind. "She killed herself just after the trial," he said flatly. "Tablets."

Marie broke the silence.

"Does anyone here doubt Dan?" Nobody did. "So what do we do with him?" she asked.

Cara, for once, found her voice. "He's not coming anywhere near my kids!" she said. A murmur of agreement rippled around.

"All in favour of banishing him immediately?" Dan said, rising.

All hands were raised.

Dan strode from the room back to Ops. He threw on his equipment and transferred the Walther to his vest, screwing on the short suppressor.

"Rich, with me," he said. Rich put on his own equipment vest, watching the cowering man at all times.

"Please!" he begged. "You've got this all wrong! I'm not a paedophile!"

"Shut your fucking mouth," snapped Dan. "I know exactly what you are; I caught you, remember?"

73

A slow veil of recognition washed over his face, quickly hidden behind more denials.

He wasted his breath.

"Your name is Kelvin Parkes. You are a convicted sex offender who should be serving a life sentence."

The man opened his mouth but couldn't speak.

Dan forced him to empty his pockets, finding an almost empty wallet. It contained a debit card in the name of Mr K L Parkes. Dan smiled triumphantly, holding the card out as further proof to the others.

"Rich, empty their car and follow us," Dan said, grabbing a roll of black duct tape and wrapping it around Kelvin's wrists roughly as he twisted them into the small of his back.

"Stop! Please!" whined Parkes pointlessly.

He was thrown in the boot of the Discovery, watched carefully by Ash from the back seat. Rich threw the handful of bags out of the car as Rob picked up his own.

"That's his," Rob said, pointing at a bag. Rich put it back in the car and drove after Dan.

They drove for nearly two hours, at times with Rich struggling to keep up. Eventually, Dan pulled up at a quarry on waste ground and got out.

He dragged Parkes from the boot and dropped him heavily onto the ground. Parkes was crying.

Dan pointed to Rich where he wanted the car. He dragged the man to his feet and slammed him against the side of his Discovery.

"Where are we?" Dan asked him.

Parkes moaned and closed his eyes tightly.

"TELL ME WHERE WE ARE," Dan screamed in his face. He drew the knife from his shoulder, seeing eyes widen in front of him. He spun Parkes around and slashed through the bindings, cutting him in the process.

Dan turned him again and hit him hard in the stomach.

As Kelvin Parkes gasped for breath in the dirt, Dan walked to Rich.

"This is where he took an eleven-year-old girl," he said. "He made friends with her through the internet. He groomed her for months, pretending he was her age. They agreed to meet up and he brought her here." He walked over and stood above him. "Tell my friend what you did to her," he said quietly.

"Please! No!" Parkes begged.

"Tell him. Now," Dan said again.

"SHE LOVED ME!" he sobbed pitifully. "They made her say those things about me!"

"She was a child. You lied to her and then you raped her. She killed herself because of you."

Dan looked at Rich, seeing silent agreement in his face.

He drew his gun, pointing it at the man's head.

"Get up," he said. "Get up and get in the car. We're letting you go."

Parkes stopped crying, barely able to believe what he had heard.

Nervously, he got to his feet and walked towards the car with the engine running, never taking his eyes off the gun.

Dan twitched the barrel at him, indicating that he should climb into the driver's seat. As Parkes got behind the wheel, Dan glanced once at Rich.

Rich nodded.

Dan stepped round and fired once into Parkes's right hand, the bullet destroying bone, tendon and ligament as it tore through his flesh. He screamed in agony and shock. Rich ran to the passenger door and shoved the car in gear as Dan forced the man's legs onto the pedals. The car went into gear and the engine howled as it revved highly.

They shut the doors, cocooning the screaming man inside the car. Dan leaned the gun into the window and shot him again in his left leg, making Parkes flinch his foot off the clutch.

The car leapt forward, hopping as it went. The momentum of the slope took the car in its inevitable grip and slowly it rolled to the cliff edge where it tipped to crash end over end into the dirty water below.

"Technically," said Rich as casually as he could as they both looked at the sinking car below them, "I saw him drive off on his own. You?"

"Yep," said Dan as he lit a cigarette with shaking hands, "rode off into the sunset all by himself. I doubt he'll be back."

They climbed back in the car, Rich to return to his peaceful day and Dan to go and avoid explaining why he hid his past from everyone.

RECOVERY

Pete's shoulder was healing slowly, helped, he claimed, by the two little spaniels who lay on his legs and seemed happy to sleep all day and all night with occasional breaks to eat or go outside. Every day, James went to him for instructions in the morning, and every evening he would sit with the old poacher and discuss his results, receiving tips and pointers based on his performance. James was putting weight on and no longer resembled the skinny, terrified kid Lexi had brought home. He had grown a sturdy set of shoulders, having taken over every heavy task from Pete. He trusted the older man, which was why, one evening, Pete told him straight that Pip didn't need him to follow her everywhere and that she was going to be fine without his help.

What Dan learned later was that the young girl had spent a long time talking with Pete, as they were the only ones being treated daily by the medical team. She had asked Pete for advice, then for his help in putting James off trying to be the husband he had never been asked to be.

James seemed to take it well, but a subtle eye was kept on him to be sure. Jack stepped in a few times a week to show him some skills and teach him about different types of animals and when their breeding seasons were.

Pete was even allowed out for a few hours at a time, which he spent fishing while sitting on a folding chair on the lake's jetty. True, he did have a fishing rod, but the only thing he ever caught seemed to be a small bottle of Scotch.

Dan didn't feel guilty about the ruse; he had discussed it with Kate beforehand, who agreed as she didn't want him sitting in medical either moping or drinking.

"It's actually not that much," she said to Dan as they discussed Pete's drinking in private one day. "He never seems to be actually drunk as such; he just needs a top-up to keep him going. I've seen way worse alcohol problems than this, and I would class Pete as 'functioning' at absolute worst."

Dan had to agree. Not once had he ever seen Pete staggering drunk, not even at Christmas when he himself had ended up throwing up in the snow, and Pete never showed any adverse signs of the alcohol affecting him. He decided to categorise Pete as "Drinker" now, and not "Alcoholic".

Marie had started to take her one day off a week to coincide with Dan's. They enjoyed a lazy lie-in which they planned ahead for and stocked his room with drinks and snacks the night before. After a morning not wasted in bed, they got up for lunch and did whatever they felt like for the rest of the day. Marie called it "pottering".

The routine had established itself well enough that on those days, Ash would spend the morning with Leah. He knew she loved the status of walking around with the huge dog at her heel. Maybe Ash would father a litter one day and she could have her own, Dan thought.

On one of their free days, Marie was restless. She wanted to go out somewhere. The irony of being a Ranger for fun on his day off from being a Ranger wasn't lost on him, but if she wanted to go out, then he would take her out.

"Where would madam like to go?" he asked lazily.

"Anywhere," she replied. "Just take me out somewhere."

He realised the furthest she had been from the house since he brought her back months ago was to the gardens where she visited Cedric and Maggie every week. "OK," he said, "but you work to my rules." He kissed her arm as they lay in bed.

She rolled over slightly so he could see her raised eyebrows. "Oh?" she asked.

"You move when I say, and you stand still when I say." He kissed her shoulder. "And you follow my instructions to the letter." He kissed her neck, making her squeak and pull away.

"You're so melodramatic!" she teased.

They dressed, and Leah reluctantly relinquished control of his dog back to him. Ash seemed unhappy too, as he probably doubted Dan would feed him anywhere near as much as Leah would.

He drove well, showing off and completely wasting his effort, as Marie didn't even notice. She was no longer the only person there who knew what Dan had been before, but she decided to push a little harder for the reasons why he was so moody at times.

She asked him to stop the car. She got out and looked around, spinning a slow circle. Dan scanned the area with his weapon, looking for dangers. He was just about to call her back to the car, to tell her to be careful, when he realised that all he ever saw nowadays was danger. He never stopped to see what she was seeing.

Now that the earth had started to claim back all the concrete and tarmac, and the busy pace of the world had replaced the rat race with the race for survival, he never stopped to appreciate the beauty around him. It was a clear day, and from the motorway flyover they had stopped on, he could see for miles. He could see three sets of hills, the two smaller ones showing the way north through a valley and a much larger range to the south. He had driven through this place so many times in his life, but never once had he seen what was beyond the line of traffic. He lowered his carbine and slowly stood up straight.

"Relax, Daniel," she said kindly.

UNBURDENED

He relaxed. He walked over to her, discarding the weapon by slinging it behind his back, and put his arms around her waist. He kissed her gently, and she responded.

They disentangled themselves and leaned back against the barrier. They lit cigarettes, and, as he exhaled slowly, she asked him the question he'd known was coming.

"What happened?" she said quietly. From all their conversations, all his attempts at diverting or distracting her, it always came back to this. She wanted to know what tortured him so much.

"Three years ago, nearly," he started, "I was a firearms officer. You know, flash car and sexy-looking kit. I was happy with life. She was in the job too. And the kids…" He stopped, swallowing down the tears which threatened. "It was a Friday night. Busy as usual. We got a call for a kid with a knife on the outskirts, bad area, you know? Concrete jungle kind of place: all high-rises, high crime rates and high unemployment."

Marie knew.

"We got there, looked around, and couldn't see anyone who looked more suspicious than normal. We'd had a lot of hoax calls there, kids on the estate throwing things at the cars. Couple of guys got hurt; one was quite bad when a freezer went over the balcony and hit a car. It was becoming an estate you didn't go onto unless you went in force."

Marie knew those areas well, having sent plenty of people in force to fetch her the bad people to lock away.

"Anyway. Walking back to the car and my mate goes down; they'd lobbed a half-brick at us from a balcony. Just dumb luck that he took it in the head. Lights out, fractured skull." He drew on his cigarette, taking it down to the end before he flicked it away with his thumb and forefinger. "A kid appears from by the car. It came to my head that they'd figured out what we were and were going to take the guns. I still believe that now, even when it doesn't matter anymore. I tried to call for backup but this kid ran at us. He had something in his hand. I couldn't see it clearly, but I was sure it was a weapon. I drew on him, shouting at the top of my voice for him to stop. He didn't, so I shot him once in the chest," he said, eyes vacant and tapping the fingers of his right hand on his sternum.

Marie stayed silent, letting Dan fill the gap.

"They all scattered," he said, looking up with tears streaming down his face. "Backup arrived and helped me do CPR on the kid. My mate survived; the kid died on scene. They took my gun, swabbed my hands, and led me away to give my initial statement; they all had that look of pity on their faces. Dead man walking." He cuffed at his eyes. "The press screamed racism. Police brutality. Black youth murdered by white cop, all that shit. He was fourteen years old. I was sure it was a gun he was carrying, but the only thing they found was his fucking phone. He was running to help, and I killed him. He wanted to be a paramedic when he grew up. He was first aid mad when all the other kids his age were chalking up robberies and weapons charges."

He cried. "It was awful. They hung me out to dry. My name got leaked and I had death threats. 'Racist pig murderer' – that's what they painted on my car. I went downhill badly. Depression, insomnia, mood swings. I was in a bad way. Not just my career. I didn't care about that anymore, but my life was over."

He looked down at the floor. "That's when she left and took the kids. I found out afterwards that she'd been dropping on her back for her boss anyway. Not that it mattered by then; everything I'd ever worked for was gone. I did my job, and the organisation crucified me for it. I was in a situation and reacted how I was taught, but it was wrong. I was wrong. Not once did the job stand up in the inquest and say I was innocent; they bent over backwards to help prove I wasn't. After eighteen months of hell, the inquiry declared a lack of any evidence to convict me for murder, but nobody forgot. It was ruled an 'accidental death following police contact'. I'd moved back to where I'd started out before transferring. Everywhere I went, it was the whispering: 'That's the bloke who shot that kid.' Bastards. You'd think your own side would look after you, wouldn't you? After that, word of the private prosecution came through. I was suspended again and was looking at a trial for manslaughter."

He paused. "It looked likely that I was going down for it." Dan angrily wiped the tears from his face and lit another cigarette. "So now you know everything," he said bitterly, "still want me around?"

Marie had stayed still and silent as it all poured out of him, and now she took a breath to speak.

He held up a hand and shushed her. She fought down her angry indignation and supressed the urge to cuff him around the head. He leapt to his feet and threw away the cigarette, calling Ash back to heel as he swung the carbine back to his front and raised it in one smooth action. He squinted through the optic pointed down the abandoned and overgrown motorway.

"What is it?" she asked, a hint of fear making her voice slightly higher than normal.

"Movement," he said gruffly. "Vehicle, almost a mile away."

HARD CHOICES

Emma nursed the uncomfortable car northwards on a motorway littered with cars and green plants overgrowing the hard shoulder and central reservation. She was sure last week that she was going to die. She had started to cough and had felt drained very quickly. She recorded her notes throughout, dictating what she felt to be her own death so that someone might find her research and the data she carried and one day understand what it was that happened to them all.

For three days, she coughed and shivered, drinking all the water she carried and being too weak to find more. She was confused, fevered. She couldn't understand how she had gone past the forty-eight-hour mark. Had she? Was she not reading her watch correctly?

She was even more confused when she woke up on the fourth day, feeling better. She had coughed so hard that her throat was sore and had bled from the minute rips caused by the violent coughing. Her abdomen hurt, and looking under her top, she saw her stomach muscles were more pronounced than ever; she found herself looking at a six-pack and wondering who it could belong to, as it couldn't be hers. She had coughed herself to death, and this was some form of afterlife. That was it.

Only it wasn't. As her mind cleared from the fever she had suffered, she realised that she had been ill but had not died. She suffered exactly the same symptoms, so she thought, but the virus had not killed her. She saw her digital voice recorder abandoned on the floor next to where she'd lain sweating and shivering. She had left it on and flattened the battery. Hopefully she could charge it in the car when she got moving again, but first she needed water.

She needed water, food and clean clothes. She had to admit she stank.

She gathered what she needed, taking aspirin to try and numb the pain in her head and body. She found clothes to wear in an abandoned shop after climbing in through the window. She washed with cold water and helped herself to deodorant and fresh clothes before leaving through a fire escape. She paused at the sign which told her that the door was alarmed, and pushed the bar anyway. She doubted there was anyone alive close enough to hear it. She started her car and continued north.

Completely unaware that she was being watched.

The two men in the car followed her. They kept back in the distance, keeping her car over a mile away when the geography allowed and waiting for the right time.

Dan whistled Ash and told him to get in. The dog launched himself through the open window of the Discovery. Dan started to walk sideways, keeping the car in his scope as he moved towards the driver's side.

"Get in, Marie," he said calmly.

"We're not going after them, are we?" she asked. "I don't... I think... Let's call up the others." She reached for the CB.

"No time," he said, and he started the big three-litre engine as she watched the car approach without the need for the optic.

"Female. Alone," he said as he reversed and went to drive down the exit slip to get behind the car. *Benefits of no traffic*, he thought. He stopped, turning the nose of the car to the left and moving to lean out of the window and raise the gun again.

"What is it?" asked Marie, flustered and more than a little annoyed at him.

He didn't answer, just reached for the CB.

"It's Dan, anyone there?" he said, keying the switch.

"Here, boss. Go," Leah snapped back efficiently after a few seconds.

Damn. "Who's there with you?" he asked.

"Just me. Lexi and Steve are off site, Rich is swimming in the lake, and Joe is sleeping off the night shift," she replied, sounding curious.

Shit, he thought. He either had to do this alone and keep Marie safe, or ask Leah to drive to find them. If she left now, she could be backing him up in ten minutes. He looked at Marie, agonising over the decision.

"Is she ready?" she asked, reading his thoughts easily.

He nodded and keyed the mic again. "Fastball op, kid. I need you to write the following down, ready?"

A second's pause, then, "Go."

He gave very succinct directions to his current location, then, "One vehicle seen, second vehicle looks to be stalking it. Suspect hostiles. I need you to back me up, get on the motorway THE WRONG WAY and follow. Take a car with a CB and go. Now."

I WON'T LET YOU DOWN

She froze for a second, letting it sink in. She threw on her vest and added the Glock and mags to it and then selected her carbine with a scope. Four magazines were charged ready, and she seated one in the weapon before adding the others to her vest. She still had the loaded Walther and a spare magazine on her left hip. She also carried a hidden sheath knife inside her trousers by her kidneys – a short blade, more of a punch knife really. The really disturbing thing about all of this was that she knew how to use them all. If any Kelvin Parkes had tried to abduct this girl, he would have been found piece by piece over the course of a few years.

She opened the cabinet where they kept the spare keys to the vehicles – those brand-new ones they had found, that was – and threw herself in Steve's Defender. She fired up the engine and accelerated hard up the driveway.

"At the motorway," came the young voice over the crackling radio.

Dan snatched up the mic. "Hard right, down the slip, then back on yourself. Go fast until you find me and then tuck in behind me," he instructed.

"Roger," came the reply.

Almost fifteen agonising minutes later, she caught sight of the back of Dan's big Discovery cruising along. She called him to say she had him in sight, and he explained what he wanted her to do.

"Next vehicle up ahead is possible hostile. Match speed and force a stop on them, then you go ahead and stop the one in front," he said.

"Confirm you want me to force stop on hostiles and then chase the other one?" she asked.

"YES," he said clearly.

"Negative. You have Marie on board. You force stop and I'll deal with hostiles," she countered.

Dan nearly threw the mic in sheer exasperation. She was right, really, and was only doing what he would do. She had tried so hard to be like him that she now was him, and he hated it. He looked at Marie for help.

"You made her a child soldier; you deal with it!" she said with amusement to cover her rising fear.

Dan shook his head at her and tried again. "Negative. You are to assist in forcing a stop and then..." He stopped talking as the vehicle in front started to speed away.

"Change of plan; we've been made. Take out hostiles now," he yelled into the radio as he accelerated hard, kicking the automatic gearbox down twice. Marie pressed herself into her seat and looked frightened. He leant over and opened the glove compartment, exposing a Sig and two spare magazines. She stared wide-eyed at him.

~

The two men in the car saw the flash of movement as the Discovery crested the rise behind them too close. They never knew that the driver was distracted by a radio argument with a young girl, but their plans were forced into early execution by the intrusion. They planned to follow her to the blockage up ahead and trap her.

Both were concerned it was some kind of government team; a second black 4x4 appeared next to the first, and they were coming hard at them. The girl still hadn't seen them as they pressed up behind her. They had been anticipating catching her ever since she went to ground somewhere last week; now that she had surfaced, their excitement had turned to fear.

Leah used the power in the gears and brought herself up level to Dan. She had the vehicle with the heavy winch bumpers, not to mention a lot less chrome than his Discovery had. She keyed the radio.

"I'll take lead and give them a nudge," she said.

It occurred to Dan that she wasn't asking: she was telling. Again, it was the best idea, as she had the vehicle which would end their pursuit of the girl instantly. He thought back to the only basis she had for this kind of thing that wasn't on the television: a demonstration using kids' toy cars on how to make contact to stop another vehicle. It was so ridiculous that she had taken such idly given information and turned it into real-world tactics.

"Do it," he said back to her.

She looked over at him and nodded before gripping the wheel tighter and pushing ahead. Dan dropped back a couple of car lengths behind her right quarter. They gained on the car quickly. As Leah got to within ten metres, the passenger window opened and a man leaned his head and shoulder out with a gun in his hand. Definitely hostile.

Leah stood hard on the accelerator and swiped her wheel to the right, hitting the smaller car in the rear doors and pushing it at an angle. She lifted off to give herself space and saw the passenger aim directly at her as their car lost control and spun. She floored the throttle, hitting the car side on and bouncing it away from her. She lifted off again before stamping down and ducking low to avoid the shot. She hit the car again and peeled off to the left as she flinched away.

She heard a metallic clang as a single round ricocheted off the roof. She glanced to her right and saw the car skidding sideways, then spin so violently back towards her that she didn't believe they could survive the crash.

The uncontrolled back end of their car had hit a stationary vehicle which was crashed nose first into the central barrier. It spun out three times before coming to a mangled stop.

Dan timed it perfectly. He saw Leah hit the car and destabilise it, then hit it again to turn it sideways. He saw her final shunt and then she peeled away, leaving the uncontrollable car to smash into the back of an abandoned Vauxhall. The car spun back around the other way, just as he timed it right to squeeze his big vehicle through the gap it left as it went. Marie screamed, and Dan tried to pretend he wasn't holding his breath.

Leah had come to a stop and was starting to reverse. She changed the plan again.

"I'll cover them. You bring the civvy back and help clear it," she said, breathless with adrenaline or fear or both. "Hurry up," she added.

"Will do," Dan answered, and he accelerated hard to hunt down the quarter-mile distance between them and the little car.

~

Emma first realised she wasn't alone when a sound behind her made her glance in the mirror. She saw a car spinning after a big crash, and through the flying debris came a big black vehicle. It got bigger in her mirror.

She panicked. Her breathing was rapid and threatened to become uncontrollable.

The car wouldn't go any faster; she tried and it just made more noise, but the speedo wouldn't go over sixty-eight miles an hour. She should've tried to find a better car.

It gained on her fast, and she knew she wouldn't get away. With one hand, she tried to get the laptop from her bag to hide it, but lost speed by doing so. The big car surged past her, pulled in front, and slowed. She tried to get past but lacked the acceleration. It was hopeless. She slowed down to stop and her mind raced with what these people would do to her. The words of the senior analyst came back to her: "You're like a hamster on a wheel. We should use you as a test subject."

She stopped and tried to prepare herself for the worst, searching the bag desperately for the gun.

Leah climbed over the passenger's seat and out of the vehicle to give herself cover. She took the gun with the scope and lay flat on the ground, watching the wrecked car. Both men were still in their seats, motionless. She forced her breathing to slow down and watched both carefully at six times magnification, watching for signs of life and waiting for help to come back.

Dan told both of his passengers to stay down and then got out and held both hands up in front of him. He kept them away from his weapons and approached slowly. He saw the young woman frantically moving before coming up with a gun pointed at him held in both hands. He was about to dive back to the cover of the vehicle but couldn't risk her firing and hitting Marie or Ash.

Leah lay flat and watched the two men. The passenger stirred, shaking the shoulder of the driver. She kept the sight over the man's head, hoping she could keep one of them alive to answer questions.

Emma panicked. She held the gun shaking in both hands and pointed it at the man who emerged from the big car. He was dressed like a soldier, and he walked slowly with his hands up. She didn't know what to do, but she was sure that she couldn't get away.

Dan kept his hands clear of the weapons, not wanting to scare the girl further; she already looked terrified.

"We've stopped the men chasing you," he said.

She was confused; she thought he was chasing her. Her mouth opened and closed, but the courage to ask anything deserted her.

"Please put that down. We're not going to hurt you. There's a young girl back there who needs my help, and the longer you fuck about, the more danger she's in," he snapped.

She wanted to trust him. She thought he seemed more annoyed than threatening.

Marie quickly grew bored of the lack of reassurance coming from her emotionally constipated partner. She carefully put the gun down on the seat and got out, walking towards the car showing her empty hands.

The girl's gun switched wildly between the two targets. Dan considered rushing forward and breaking the window, but now couldn't risk Marie getting hurt.

"Please," Marie called out, "we can help you."

Dan took another step forward as the girl's grip on the gun faltered. Just as he heard two gunshots pierce the air.

Leah watched him try to wake the driver, then give up and force the mangled door open. It was twisted and bent where she had rammed into the passenger's side, and he had to kick out to give himself space to escape. He fell to the floor on all fours and looked around, his eyes resting on her Land Rover. He had a big, heavy-looking automatic handgun in his right hand and was dressed all in black similar to herself.

He raised himself up, dazed by the impact, and pointed the gun at her.

She fired, hitting him in the lower leg – an easy shot through her scope. He spun to the floor, pulling the trigger and sending a harmless bullet into the air as he fell. She stayed in position, silently willing her hero and mentor to come back. The scream seemed to take an age to escape the man's mouth, the shock of the pain making it build until it finally escaped and tore the air.

Dan couldn't see Leah or the car from where he was, and he shot a pleading look at Marie.

"Go," she said to him.

He had to trust that the girl was not a threat, just scared. He threw himself behind the wheel and turned around to launch the big 4x4 towards Leah.

The seconds it took to cover the ground felt like minutes, and he pulled up short to get out. He left Ash in the car with the door open, telling him to stay. Taking cover behind a vehicle and raising his carbine, he called out to his protégé. "Leah!" he yelled.

"Here," came the instant reply, easily heard over twenty metres. "Driver's out of it; passenger armed with one in the leg. Covering," she called back, not taking her eye off the bleeding, writhing man.

Dan moved up along the central reservation, keeping the car visible over his weapon and seeking cover from the side where the passenger was.

At five metres away, he slowed, sidestepping to his right to get a view of the injured man. Dan stepped in quickly, kicking the gun away from him.

"Move up," Dan called to Leah.

Leah abandoned the G36 where it was, drawing the Glock from the holster on her chest with a well-practised hand. She rounded the front of her vehicle and took a line of cover to stand behind Dan, all the while keeping the immobile driver in her sights. The hours of practice showed as they performed their contact drills in silence.

She tapped Dan on the back, and he slung his carbine to grab the man she had wounded. Dan dragged him up and held him against the side of the car, looking for more weapons and spare ammunition for the gun. The bleeding man said nothing and kept his eyes screwed shut. Dan put him back on the ground and moved to the driver's side. Leah automatically switched her aim to cover the man Dan had searched.

Dan drew the Walther and went to open the driver's door, finding it similarly wedged from the impact. He took his finger off the trigger and smashed the window using the butt of the gun. The driver didn't move as the beads of broken glass cascaded over him; *little wonder*, Dan thought as he saw the huge injury to the right side of the driver's head. The skull was crushed on one side just above his ear from the impact, and it leaked blood slowly.

Dan nodded to Leah and went to the injured man. He was groggy from the crash, and the bullet that passed through his calf had taken enough blood from him to make his face pale.

"Who are you? Why were you after the girl?" Dan asked. He received no reply other than the man opening his eyes and staring straight through him. "Who are you?" he asked again, more forcefully.

He smiled, dribbling blood from his mouth, and said in a heavily accented voice, "Fuck you" before his eyes closed and his head sagged. Dan checked for a pulse, finding him alive for now. He left him where he was.

"Good work, kid, really good," he said to Leah, prompting a smile of pride.

A noise made him look up, and he saw the little car heading back to them. Marie drove and the girl sat in the passenger's seat, hugging her bag with eyes wide as she saw the mess in front of her, still gripping the gun tightly.

They stopped, and the girl stared at the carnage in front of her. She glanced at Leah and visibly did a double take at the child.

"These men were chasing you," said Dan. "Any idea why?"

She shook her head slowly, unable to tear her gaze away from the pool of blood on the ground.

"Dan, this is Emma," Marie said. On hearing her name, Emma snapped out of her trance and looked at him. "And this is Leah," Marie finished.

Leah kept her gaze over the sights of her gun still trained on the unconscious man, but said "'sup," trying to sound cool and succeeding.

Emma didn't recognise the men, nor did she know why they were coming after her.

"We'll take him back for questioning. Marie, can you drive mine with Emma?" Dan said.

Marie nodded, but the girl woke up from her daze again.

"No! I've got to keep going!" she said, almost believing it herself.

"Fine, but rest with us and go on after with supplies and a better car," Dan said.

Emma didn't think she had much of a choice, and in the back of her mind she longed for a conversation with anyone but herself.

Marie sealed the deal. "Hot showers," she said, leaving the rest to Emma's imagination.

Emma shuffled off to the big car and let out a small scream as she saw a huge dog in the window displaying rows of big, sharp teeth. Marie gently reached out and took the gun from Emma's unresisting hands.

"Ash, heel!" Dan said with a smile, and Ash slunk out of the open door to stand by his feet.

"Watch him," he said quietly, pointing at the unconscious man. Ash turned a snarl on him, adding a snap of his teeth but getting no response.

Dan turned to the adult women and nodded. "Leah can take me back with him."

They went, and Dan dragged the man to the boot of Leah's car, Ash following ready to attack if given permission or if he moved. Dan sat in the back, keeping a careful eye and a gun on their prisoner as Leah drove. He had a worry that this man was more than averagely dangerous.

FIRST RANGER'S QUESTION TIME

He told Leah to drive to the farm, a sadistic but effective idea forming in his head.

They pulled in and she went to search for Chris. Dan told him what he wanted, adding, "You've read *Silence of the Lambs*?"

Chris had, and he looked puzzled – even a little disturbed – but knew well enough not to ask now.

Dan stripped the man and tied his black shirt tight around the ragged bullet hole in his leg. That got a pain response.

The naked man was tipped into a wheelbarrow and taken to a small shed where a litter of last year's pigs ran. He tied him up and waited. He got bored of waiting and threw a bucket of dirty water in the man's face, forcing him back into consciousness.

Dan kicked him lightly in his wounded leg and stood back as the cry of pain became a murderous look aimed directly through him. Definitely more than averagely dangerous.

"Why were you chasing that girl?" Dan asked.

"Go fuck your mother," the man said helpfully.

"I don't have the time right now; I'm too busy about to fuck you instead," Dan retorted in an annoyingly calm manner. The man responded with a fairly legible rant about England, Dan, and his mother again, along with other various subjects which rapidly bored him. He even threatened Dan with what would happen when he got out of his current predicament, before he lapsed back into his native language to better continue the obscenities.

Dan sighed, explaining that he obviously wasn't going to untie him just so he could try and escape and have to have his arse handed to him a second time today. "Only this time it won't be done by a thirteen-year-old girl," he said with a smile, and stepped close. "I do hope you can understand me properly," he said as he leaned in closer to him. "I'm going to really, really hurt you unless you tell me what I want to know. If you do, you might get a doctor. If you don't, I'll keep going until you die. Up to you."

The man probably understood him, because he spat at Dan's face.

That was a mistake: Dan could handle being punched, shot at, stabbed, but he really disliked spitters.

He hit him in the body with four hard punches in quick succession, alternating hands as he did.

He stepped back, waiting for the man to catch his breath and abuse him again. He suddenly remembered that Leah was still there watching and thought to send her away. He didn't; it wasn't like he could remove any more of her childhood, as there was probably nothing left. The only reason he had someone to interrogate was because she'd had the foresight to intentionally wound him. If she had wanted to from that distance, she could have put bullets through both eyes.

The head rose again, and Dan didn't wait for the next volley of obscene abuse. He stepped in and delivered another series of stinging blows. The man hung limply again, catching his breath.

Twice more Dan did that, trying to establish a pattern in the man's head that this wouldn't stop, no matter what he said. That way he wouldn't bother keeping anything back. That was the theory, anyway.

Dan decided on a different approach as his impatience got the better of him, selecting a pronged fork for moving straw which he used to poke at the bullet wound, drawing screams of agony.

"You're going to die of infection, and these pigs are going to eat you," Dan said nastily.

"No more! Please!" the man said.

Dan asked him again. He gave his answers in gasps, his breath ragged from the beatings, finally giving up their intentions when Leah ended their pursuit.

"We follow her, waiting for her to hit roadblock."

"What else?" he asked, raising the pitchfork again.

"NO! I tell you everything!" he screamed.

Dan doubted that, but he'd at least removed his suspicions that the girl was different to any other vulnerable survivor.

Still, there was just something not right about her; she seemed too... new.

THE SCIENTIST

The prisoner was shut in a room on the farm. Chris watched the door until Dan got back to the house and sent Joe up to take over. Dan would have to deal with him soon, but not before he had found out more. He wanted to ask the new girl her story before his suspicion got the better of him.

He walked into the house with Leah and Ash. He left Leah in Ops cleaning her carbine and full of pride, giving Ash a bowl of food and telling him to stay with her.

She did well today, he thought. He walked into the dining room looking for the new arrival, instead finding Marie with a hot drink.

"Where is she?" he barked.

Marie was not amused with his tone, and her face let him know that.

"Hello. Where's the new girl?" he said patiently with a smile and a tone of voice which showed far more deference.

Marie thought that was better. "She's showering. She hasn't had hot water in weeks."

"What did she tell you?" Dan asked, trying to get as much background as he could until he could speak to her.

"She was in a facility down south somewhere, underground. Some kind of shelter, I presume. The power ran out and they went outside; she's heading for Scotland. That's all she said," Marie told him.

"Something's not right," he said, sitting down opposite her. "Up for a little tag-team interview with her?"

Emma stood under the hot water, letting it soak through her greasy hair and wash the film of dried sweat from her skin. She scrubbed herself clean twice over, letting the fear of the previous weeks rinse down the plug with the soapy water. She shaved and washed until she started to feel human again.

She dried herself with a clean towel and dressed in the clean clothes they had given her. She picked up her bag before walking out of the bathroom, making her way back downstairs. Cara had laid out a selection of food, making her forget her normal hang-ups about people seeing her eat. She ate hungrily, savouring real food again. When she had finished, the man she had pointed a gun at earlier stood and offered her coffee. It tasted good.

"So, Emma," said the blonde woman, Marie, smiling, "tell us about yourself."

She paused, wondering why she felt the need to be secretive about her plans.

"It's OK," said the man, "we've all of us got a past, but something tells me yours is a little different."

What did he know? She glanced at her bag, then back to them. Dan resisted the urge to reach over and snatch the rucksack away and find out for himself.

"I need a plug point," Emma said quietly, "to be able to show you properly."

The three of them went to Ops, where the laptop was plugged in and started its slow warm-up. She took her voice recorder and connected it to the USB port.

"I was involved in a virology research programme as part of my doctorate," she said. "When word first reached us that an epidemic was spreading, they moved all of our research and most of the team into a facility in the city. There were others – politicians and military." Her eyes glazed over.

Marie prompted her to continue.

"Most people sent to our site didn't get in; it was only really the first ones who weren't infected. We locked down and watched the world fall apart from the CCTV monitors, but we lost power in the end." She spoke softly, slowly, like it was all becoming real to her just now. "Eventually the solar power and the generator fuel ran out, and we had to leave. It was never designed to hold out indefinitely without being able to go topside. We left, and everyone got sick and died. Except me." She decided not to mention the Colonel and his breakdown; she didn't want to have to justify out loud leaving a human being to die.

"What's in Scotland?" asked Dan.

"The main virology research centre. It's a top-secret thing; even my team didn't know about it until we spoke to them in the bunker. We lost contact with them too," she said sadly, suddenly feeling very tired. "I was hoping I could get there and find out what this is. I have a theory, but you might not like it," she finished as she typed in a long password to log on to the computer.

"Go on," Marie urged her gently.

"This pathogen is very fast-acting. The gestation period to fatality is the quickest of all known lethal infections ever. It's like Spanish Flu on steroids," she explained as she turned the computer to show coloured graphs depicting something which Dan lacked the patience to comprehend.

Get to the point, he thought irritably. "So?" he asked when no further explanation came.

"So I think it IS Spanish Flu on steroids. Don't you see?" She brought up another chart showing times between exposure, symptoms becoming visible, and death. "Nothing natural should be this lethal so quickly, but there must be a random element of natural immunity. How are we all still alive? I see no obvious genetic theme running in all of the survivors, so why didn't we die?"

Dan hoped the questions were rhetorical, as she was starting to lose him a little. "So what are you saying?" he asked. "In simple terms."

"I'm saying we were attacked. I believe this to be an airborne biological weapon. Possibly," she said with resounding finality.

Dan's mind swam with ideas and theories as he walked back to the farm. Joe had taken over watching the unconscious attacker. Dan had talked with Marie about what to do with him, not necessarily open to ideas other than putting him down. It was Leah who pointed out that he had been bound, blindfolded and mostly unconscious when they brought him back, and that he had only seen the inside of a shed while there.

Dan agreed that he didn't need to die, but dumping him somewhere with a bullet hole in his leg would be worse than killing the man himself. He cleaned and dressed the wound, giving the man back his clothes and adding a bottle of antibiotic tablets. His hands were tied behind his back and he was blindfolded again before being put in the boot of Dan's Discovery, then driven around for over twenty miles of aimless driving just to confuse him before he was taken back to where his dead friend sat in the wrecked car. He was handed the keys to the small vehicle Emma had been driving and told very firmly that if he was ever seen by them again, they would kill him.

The man drove south without looking back.

SCIENCE TRIP

Emma agreed to stay for a while and recover her strength, as her recent illness had left her weak. Marie called a council meeting that night and explained what had happened with Emma and what she had said afterwards.

The news of an attack using biological weapons being a possibility didn't really affect any of them, which frustrated Dan.

"If this is a bioweapon, don't you see the implications?" he asked the blank faces staring at him. "If we've been attacked by another country, ask yourselves *why?*"

Nobody spoke.

"What if it's a precursor to invasion?" he suggested to them, finally getting some hint in their faces that they were beginning to grasp the point. "We have no idea if any other countries are affected by it; it could simply be that the island has been quarantined."

"Slight problem with that theory," offered Neil. "If there were still other people, other intact governments, out there in the world, then why haven't we seen any aircraft?"

Dan thought about that one. He hadn't seen anything in the sky that hadn't evolved to fly in almost a year, not even a faint vapour trail. He assumed that if they were under quarantine, there would at least be some kind of reconnaissance flight higher up, or even a broadcast on the radio.

"Granted," Dan said, "so the other possibilities are that we've been attacked and are going to see Chinese tanks or whoever heading down the driveway soon, or that the whole world is affected."

"It doesn't really matter what we think, though, does it?" said Chris quietly. "How are we going to know for sure?"

Dan took a breath and told them of the conversation he and Marie had had with their newest guest. "Emma wants to go to some lab in Scotland where they test stuff like this. She said she might be able to say whether the virus is synthetic or not."

There was silence in the room as each considered the benefits.

"But what would the point be?" asked Chris again. "How will it affect us?"

"Honestly? I don't know, but it may give us some answers. I think there's no harm in helping her," Dan said, waiting for the next question.

"Help her how?" said Marie.

"She'll need a vehicle and supplies. I also think she should have an escort." He left it there.

"Who?" said Marie, worrying what the answer would be.

"I don't know yet," said Dan carefully. "It would have to be a Ranger, obviously, and it would be their choice to go." This meant that it would probably be him.

"Shall we bring the other Rangers in?" Marie enquired.

"Please let me speak to them first," Dan replied. "Shall we meet tomorrow?"

He sat at the table in Ops, having asked Leah to shut the door. The door hadn't been shut since the day they found the house.

Dan finished the explanation and let the silence hang heavy. The same questions were floated around the table, and they weighed the benefits and risks of the journey.

"It's not like a cure is an issue; there's very few of us left," said Steve. "Knowing if it was deliberate or nature redressing some kind of imbalance is academic, surely?"

Lexi agreed – better to forget the past and concentrate on the future, she felt.

Still, something in the back of Dan's mind wanted to know more about what had happened to them.

"Are none of you interested to know if it's the same everywhere? What if we're the only ones affected?" he asked them.

He sensed something from them, more nervous than apathetic.

"She wants to go, and I won't stop her," Dan said, "but she has a better chance of surviving the trip and bringing back answers if she has an escort. She didn't even know she was being chased when we found her, for God's sake!"

"I'd go, but you probably won't let me," Leah offered.

"Correct," said Steve, "you're not going. I will." He looked directly at Dan and repeated himself. "I'll go."

"OK," Dan said, seeing the relief on the faces of Lexi and Joe.

"Get me the location," said Leah. "I'll start looking at a route."

They went to find Emma to tell her what they had decided. She accepted the news quietly, shaking Steve's hand as they were formally introduced.

"I want to give you the best chance of making it there, so that's why Steve is going to take you," said Dan. "Also, I'd like you to do some training with us so that you know what to do in different situations. Chances are the journey north will be dangerous; without us, it's highly unlikely you'll make it there. Sorry to sound blunt, but it's the truth."

Emma accepted this and asked when they would leave. Steve said it would take a week to prepare properly.

Emma closed the laptop and stood, indicating her readiness to start straight away.

Steve led Emma off to begin survival 101 after Dan asked for the location of the facility. He gave this to Leah as he passed, taking Steve's Defender to Neil's workshop on the farm.

An oil-stained Neil looked up from where he was buried in the engine of a tractor, with the diminutive Ewan assisting in replacing whatever part had failed.

They greeted Dan warmly, giving the sense of being men happy in their work.

Dan told him what he wanted, making Neil's brain spin with the possibilities and problems.

"Extra fuel tank up top," he suggested, pointing to the roof rack. "I'll have to strip the rear seats to make space for spare wheels and tools, but they'll still have to travel fairly light."

"Not a problem," said Dan. "How long do you reckon?"

Neil thought for a while and said five days. Dan knew he meant three; he just wanted to look good getting it done ahead of time. He thanked him and walked back to the house with Ash.

THE MISSION

Steve had been thorough with Emma's training. She was well equipped and he had given her basic weapon training with a pistol for worst-case self-defence situations. She packed and repacked her equipment until he was happy that she could save no more weight.

Neil had done well. Steve's Defender had been thoroughly serviced and checked before the retrofitting had begun, and it now had a large heavy plastic reservoir tank on the roof rack. Neil's estimate that it held enough fuel for another five hundred miles was probably generous, but he had included a hand pump to fill the two charged jerrycans fitted inside the rear door. The roof tank had a large opening on top which could be refilled with ease, and he had brimmed it with the slightly pink-tinged liquid from the agricultural tank.

Four spare wheels were strapped down behind the rear seats, with almost half of the boot space left for their equipment. He had even patched the bullet score mark above the windscreen.

Evidence of Leah's interception marked the front bumper with minor dents and scratches, but having hit the soft skin of a car with the heavy steel bumper left nothing more than cosmetic damage.

He brought the heavy off-roader down to the house, sporting its nine wheels and almost thousand-mile fuel range.

Steve emerged carrying heavy bags. He was armed with his sidearm and M4 and had a vest stocked well with spare magazines. He also took an Mk14 and an additional handgun which was stashed in the glove compartment. Emma had been equipped with a ballistic vest and sturdy clothing. Both carried minimal personal equipment, with camp cots and sleeping bags to complement their small stove and box of tinned food. They took plenty of water, anticipating a few weeks away at worst.

Emma cleared her throat nervously. "Can I ask one more favour?" she asked the small assembled group.

Dan invited her to proceed.

"I have collected blood samples from the people I was underground with, after they showed signs of infection." Her voice dropped into uncertainty before she took a breath and raised her head. "To be able to have other samples to test against, I need – I'd like if you would allow me to take samples from some of you," she finished.

Awkward silence hung over the gathering until Dan took the lead and rolled up his left sleeve. "I'll go first," he announced, prompting half a dozen people to follow suit and file into the medical wing.

They left after breakfast with no ceremony, everyone acting as though it were a normal trip out to try and convince themselves.

Steve drove steadily, weaving the heavy Defender through the overgrown roads. In places, what used to be two wide lanes had become a single tunnel between the hedges grown wild in the spring. Leah had done well with their route; she had marked a series of roads snaking north with alternative loops in places. Their journey was engineered to avoid the major population centres and to keep off the motorways through the most built-up areas. It would not be a quick drive, but it should minimise the risks they had to take.

Steve found Emma to be a quiet, nervous girl. In truth, she was no girl, and close to finishing her doctorate, although still half his own age. He didn't mind; he liked silence, and she didn't have much to say for the first day. He didn't feel the need to fill the void with unnecessary talking, and she didn't ask questions. His job was to get them there, and she couldn't help much with that. Her job was at the lab.

They moved onwards, Emma lost in her thoughts and theories and Steve concentrating on the road ahead.

ROADBLOCKS

Three times on the first day they had to double back and take alternative loops. It was easy enough to avoid the blockages, but after the third time, Steve's impatience and tiredness got to him. He had been concentrating all day and they had barely made more than a hundred miles.

Emma was some help reading the maps, but she wasn't a navigator by any means; she was more used to negotiating underground train maps than planning a route by car. He had to stop and check it himself a few times, conscious not to let his annoyance show through as he did so.

As the sun started to set, Steve called a stop to the day and cleared a small building on a higher patch of ground off the road. Emma had still barely said two words since they had left, not that he took offence to her manner. As Steve set up the camping cooker and began to erect his cot, she broke her silence and asked for help.

She caught her finger and swore loudly, dropping the half-made bed as she hopped around, holding her hand. Steve smiled at her misfortune.

"It's not bloody funny!" she admonished him.

"I'm sorry. I shouldn't laugh. Here," he replied, helping her put the square poles in the right order. He finished the bed easily and she sat on the taut canvas heavily, tired from a day sitting in a car concentrating.

"I had never even slept outside of a proper bed until the bunker," she said, head in her hands as she rubbed her face.

"Never too old to experience something new," Steve said, instantly regretting sounding so contrite. He busied himself heating the water for a hot drink as she got up and wandered around, looking at the old contents of the shelves in their temporary shelter.

"I wondered about this kind of thing for years," she said distantly.

Steve had never heard her speak other than to ask or answer direct questions, so his interest was piqued by her sudden daydreaming. "About camping in a derelict shop with an ageing helicopter pilot?" he asked, attempting to lighten the mood.

"No," she said, running a finger along the packets containing long-ago-spoiled food. "About what would happen with a virus or something like this. It was all numbers and theories: infectivity ratios, urban population versus rural survival rates, developing algorithms to predict the spread..." She trailed off as she walked slowly, bringing her back to her cot. "That kind of thing. I never once actually considered what it would have been like to survive day by day without modern comforts." She stopped, fixing her gaze directly on him. "Without fast food and the Internet, most people would just fade away!" she said with a smile, bringing herself out of her daydream with levity to detract from her darker thoughts.

"They surely would," agreed Steve, decanting hot water into two mugs and replacing it on the cooker to add packets of instant noodles.

The regular silence lowered its veil over them for the rest of the evening. They ate, they walked away quietly to tend to their own personal needs, and they lay in their cots after darkness settled with no conversation other than to wish each other a customary goodnight.

The next four days went by very similarly. Some days they made more distance, others far less. They found places of interest on the journey north, and Steve took the opportunity to top up his fuel despite not having had to use the large reserve tank on the roof yet. Emma offered to drive once, and Steve accepted to give his body a rest from the constant position behind the wheel.

She crunched the gears and her clutch control was so ineffective that Steve's back hurt more in the passenger's seat. Despite their lack of conversation, he felt comfortable enough in her company to offer his opinion about it.

"Do you actually know how to drive?" he asked after they nudged the kerb for no reason for the third time.

"Yes! I just haven't been behind the wheel much since I learned how," she admitted reluctantly.

He took back the controls as soon as it was polite to do so. He tried to explain that he wasn't being chauvinistic about it, but was more worried for the fuel consumption and the possible damage to the car. The more he explained, the more he felt himself sinking into the hole he was digging. He gave up and they fell back into their normal quiet routine.

After six days and not a single soul seen, they crossed over the border into Scotland.

ROYAL VISIT

Pat thought long and hard about how to go about his business. He considered sending some of his boys in to be "rescued" by them, conjuring up elaborate plans of showing resistance with a gun battle so they were more inclined to trust his moles. He dismissed that; the accuracy and savagery of the shooting aimed at them when just one of them came still echoed in his thoughts.

Maybe just a straightforward visit? Stroll up and knock on the front door – a bit of civility cost nothing. His new chief scout had told him about two other vehicles like the one which had come to his land – he had to assume that meant another two armed similarly and just as dangerous. He didn't have the hardware to counter that; true, he had lots of guns, but they were all hunting tools and not military-grade like those he had faced.

He didn't want to risk a conflict with this group, as he had no idea how many of them there were, but he couldn't allow their incursion to go unchallenged. Rules must be agreed and compensation paid.

"Load up, boys!" he shouted, sparking a series of flurried movements as the nearest of his subjects scrambled to their feet. "We're going to visit the English!"

~

Dan gave up on trying to keep Leah off the front line. She was undoubtedly capable, but he still worried that she was far too young to go out alone. He was teaching her how to use the heavy-calibre battle rifle one morning – not that she required much instruction after Steve's thorough lessons. She had mastered using the automatic carbine in a day, and followed suit with a suppressor and scope like Dan's. Her M4 was painted in a dappled camouflage colour, and she cherished it more than she used to cherish her phone.

He realised how quickly he had become accustomed to seeing her armed. Before it happened, the thought of a child carrying guns was abhorrent to him – even more so because of his personal experiences – but seeing her emulate him was flattering, and he felt a genuine pride in her abilities. The scared little girl was long gone. In her place stood a fierce and fit young woman, the next generation of their leadership.

Dan had decided that if he was going to have to rely on her to cover him, he preferred it if she was firing either lots more or heavier rounds. They took turns firing five rounds each from the battle rifle into a large tree at about four hundred metres, and Leah matched his accuracy easily. At half that distance, she joked that she could draw a smiley face.

Engine noise pierced the edge of their hearing, rendering both of them quiet just as Ash sat up from where he lay flat, turning his head towards the source. The noise was wrong. It wasn't the heavy metallic sounds of their own diesels, but the higher-pitched note of a petrol engine. More notes joined the first, until it sounded like a small swarm of bees were headed their way. They ran back to the house and as they neared the drive, Dan handed back the heavy rifle he had carried and silently pointed Leah up to one of the solar panel towers.

He stood his ground in the middle of the drive fifty metres in front of the house and fired the ugly shotgun twice into the air.

Seconds later, Rich ran from the house with a rifle in hand; he dropped to one knee by the treeline to Dan's left and asked what was going on.

"Engines, not ours. Sounds like quite a few, and they're coming our way. I need the gardens and the farm on lockdown and everyone armed," Dan said as he scanned the limits of his vision through his scope.

Rich ran back to the house without another word, no doubt getting straight on the CB radio. Lexi and Joe were off site, but Joe was still in radio range and turned around to head home in support.

Noises of activity started to grow behind Dan, indicating that others were arming themselves and preparing for whatever came their way. Rich sprinted back to him, now wearing a vest filled with spare magazines.

"Jack's on the radio. Where do you want me?" Rich asked.

"Farm. If they come down there, then put an ambush in on the driveway. I've got Leah up top with a heavy rifle," Dan replied, pointing towards Leah's nest.

Rich nodded and ran in a wide loop to the right, making cross-country to the farm as Dan sent Ash into the trees to hide.

The noises of engines grew louder until Dan could clearly make out different notes before the sight that unfolded made his mouth drop open.

A large black car rolled down the drive, surrounded by six motorcycles positioned as outriders. It was an unintentional parody of a travelling dignitary: a farce in the ruins of their old lives. Dan would have laughed had he not been so shocked and on edge at the intrusion.

He made a show of slowly racking the bolt on his weapon before settling it into his shoulder and taking a sideways stance. He was conscious not to point the gun at them, but held it ready enough to raise it if needed. He hoped that the message was clear enough.

The ridiculous motorcade came to rest twenty metres from him as the driver got out and made a show of looking around before he opened the rear door. Very Secret Service, but he completely failed to notice the young girl pointing a rifle at him which was capable of tearing through the roof and killing the important passenger without even seeing him.

Amateurs, thought Dan, all for show.

The passenger got out. Dan was presented with a fat man wearing a suit with the most pretentious thing he had ever seen on his head: the man was wearing a crown. The fake Secret Service agent strode forward, complete with sunglasses, and stood in front of Dan.

"I present the King of Wales. You will address him as 'Your Majesty'," he commanded.

"Will I? Well, you can bugger off and go talk into your sleeve, sunshine," Dan replied. He was not in the mood to be dictated to on his own doorstep.

His Majesty King Patrick took the reins. "No need for unpleasantness," boomed the self-made sovereign as he stepped forward and offered Dan a hand.

"Patrick," he said, "King of Wales."

Dan ignored the hand and tightened the grip on his carbine. "What's your business here, Fagin?" Dan said.

He dropped his hand and boomed a laugh. "Do I need a reason to visit a neighbouring country and offer the hand of friendship?"

"Let me tell you what I know," Dan said carefully. "A while ago, one of my lot fired on your ambush and rescued four women who didn't want to be part of your happy gang. With that in mind, you can see why I'm a little sceptical about you being here."

King Patrick's face dropped, all semblance of joviality abandoned. "You forgot that one of yours killed one of mine in cold blood," he said acidly.

"Regrettable but unavoidable," replied Dan equably. "If you don't want more bloodshed, I suggest you turn around and fuck off over the border, pal."

Pat sneered. "What's to stop me cutting you down right here?" he said nastily as he opened his suit jacket and exposed a gun in his waistband.

Dan slowly took his hands away from his weapon, drew himself up to his full height and smiled.

"Nothing," he said. "Only that you wouldn't live long enough to drag that toy past your gut. HEEL," he snapped to his left without taking his eyes from the man. Ash prowled forwards, head low and teeth exposed in a silent snarl. To make his point more firmly, Dan glanced very deliberately up to his right and back to the intruder.

Pat tore his eyes away from the savage animal watching him and glanced in the direction of the scaffolding tower. From a distance of less than thirty metres, the sound of a heavy bullet slowly being racked into a chamber was unmistakable.

"And we're just the ones you can see," Dan said. "If you tried anything now, and by some miracle survived, then the way out is far more dangerous than you could imagine. So leave now and forget any ideas you have about taking us on."

Pat was many things, but he was not stupid. He relaxed and brought back the genial smile from before as he waved to his group to relax. "How about we just talk, then?" he said.

"Your lot stay here. No weapons inside," Dan said.

Pat removed his handgun, as did his bodyguard. "If they move from the car, they will be shot. Please make that clear to them," he finished.

He looked to Leah, who raised a thumb to tell him that she had overheard and understood. Dan walked to the house, and at the front door he turned to face his two uninvited guests.

"Hold your arms out," he instructed them.

Pat smiled and complied as Dan ran deft hands over him, checking for weapons. The bodyguard wasn't happy and started to protest being searched.

"Fine," snapped Dan, "stay out here with him." He pointed to Ash as he muttered, "Watch him." The dog's sudden snarling was encouragement enough for the man to hold his arms out and stand very still. Dan took a knife from the man's waistband and dropped it on the floor outside.

"What about your weapons?" the bodyguard summoned up the courage to ask.

Dan turned to him. "My roof, my rules," he said with finality before leading them inside. People were moving around, some carrying shotguns. Dan walked into the lounge area and nodded to Marie to stay before loudly asking to have the room.

FOREIGN RELATIONS

The four sat in silence for a while until His Majesty King Patrick asked an audacious question. "No coffee?" he said with a smile.

"You won't be staying long enough," replied Dan. "State your business."

Patrick sighed, annoyed at missing the opportunity to observe the proprieties. "Seems to me that we need to discuss borders, among other things," he began.

"Simple," said Marie, rapidly picking up on exactly who this man wearing a ridiculous gold circlet was. "We don't cross into Wales and you don't cross into England."

Patrick shook his head. "It's not quite that simple, my love," he began.

Marie's anger flashed, putting the fat pretender firmly in his place. "Do not walk into my house and patronise me," she snapped savagely as she stood to tower over him. "I see a very clear solution: you call yourself the King of Wales, so you have Wales and we won't encroach. You are not in any position to dictate terms otherwise. I will happily provide details of the fates of people who have threatened us here if you would like?"

Her outburst silenced the man. His bodyguard looked nervous; he doubted he had any chance of competing with the man sitting opposite him even if he was unarmed and the huge dog watching his every move unsettled him greatly. Outgunned and outclassed, he felt it best to keep silent.

Patrick seemed to realise that he shouldn't push the issue. "I meant no offence, my lo–" he stopped himself before he invited another tirade from the steely woman, "madam. I merely wish to establish firm rules to prevent further clashes between our nations."

"Agreed. You stay in your country and we shall stay in ours. I can't see any way we would clash as long as that is observed," she said more calmly. "Now, tell us how you knew where to find our home."

Patrick sat back and grinned with smug satisfaction. "My eyes and ears have a long reach," he bragged magnanimously.

"So one of your feral children followed my Ranger back undetected," said Dan. "We're more than capable of returning the favour. We paid a visit to a group we didn't like recently. I'd say you could ask them how it went, but you'd need a séance." He left it there, the threat hanging heavily.

"Fine," said Patrick. "We keep to our own and you do the same, but that doesn't mean we have to be enemies."

"What are you proposing?" Marie asked.

"We aren't animals, despite what the women you brought back told you. We need more women to have babies, and we've suffered miscarriages and a stillbirth since this all started. We're not unlike yourselves, honestly," he said unconvincingly.

Dan reckoned that they probably were just how he thought. He wanted breeders. "If you suggest for one second that we give you women, you're out of your bloody mind. We don't run a dictatorship here; we look after our people and don't force them to do things they don't want to. We still have our humanity."

Marie stood. "Thank you for the visit, but we will not trade with your group, nor will you take anyone from us. Goodbye," she said with finality.

"There's still the matter of compensation to be discussed," Patrick announced in a commanding tone. "The death of one of my boys and the destruction of three cars."

"Compensation?" asked Dan incredulously.

Patrick nodded, wobbling his jowls and the ludicrous crown as his head moved.

"No. There will be no compensation. You can go now, but you had better not consider coming back."

Pat wasn't so easily dissuaded. "All I ask is for some weapons to defend ourselves," he blurted out, all confidence gone.

"To bully and steal, you mean," Marie bit back.

"I have a rule: I never put a gun in the hands of anyone I don't trust. I don't trust you," Dan said simply.

"You can leave now," said Marie, turning her back and walking out.

Dan smiled and gestured with his arm the way to the front door. A deflated King and his useless bodyguard shuffled out, marked every step by Ash and followed by Dan. The bodyguard nervously stopped to retrieve his knife, still watched by the big dog. Dan considered telling Ash to leave him but decided to let the dog enjoy himself. Ash was a killer, but he also enjoyed his amateur dramatics.

Dan followed them to their car, and as Patrick was walking to the rear door, he spoke softly to him. "Tell them whatever you like to save face, but seriously, don't come back. We have over seventy people and I can arm more than half of them. Don't think you can take us on, because you can't. We want to be left alone, and trust me, you don't want us to have to come calling."

Patrick looked at him and nodded once. He sat down heavily in the back of the car and breathed out a long sigh of defeat. He had come expecting his royal status to carry weight, only to find a larger group of people who were far better equipped and organised than his own. He had showed his hand and found himself facing better cards. Luckily, he had gambled nothing on this round, and doubted he could afford to sit down at the green cloth again.

HOLD YOUR FIRE!

Steve threw himself behind the engine block of an abandoned car and screamed at Emma to get down.

Rounds pinged and whined off the metal as three or four people shot at his hiding place.

"STOP SHOOTING!" he bellowed. Three times he repeated this until he heard shouts and voices coming from the blocked road ahead. He had got out to see if he could force a way through or drag clear an obstruction using the winches on his Land Rover, but the way was thoroughly blocked. Almost deliberately so, he thought, just as the first shot tore the air. It probably wasn't intended to hit him, but that made little difference when being fired at.

Emma had ducked down in the footwell of the truck, despite Steve's instructions to never hide in a vehicle if someone shoots at you. They ignored her, concentrating their fire on his position until they finally relented.

"What do you want?" came the faint shout in an unmistakably Scottish accent.

"We just want to get past. We'll go another way, just please don't bloody shoot!" he responded, blood pumping hard around his body.

"Put down your guns," came the instruction.

Steve was annoyed. He had brought enough weaponry to cope with losing his personal weapons, but it was a matter of principle not to allow himself to be robbed. "We mean you no harm; we are literally passing through. We don't want any trouble!" he shouted back from his hiding place.

"Hands in the air and come out now," shouted a new voice, this one closer and full of authority.

Steve held both hands up and slowly rose with the carbine dangling on its sling. He saw a big man in green camouflage pointing a military rifle at him. Everything about him – his clothes, his stance, his voice – made Steve think he was a trained soldier. He tried a new approach.

"I'm Flight Lieutenant Steven Bennett of the Royal Air Force," he declared, standing tall and investing his words with an entitlement which bordered on arrogance.

The man responded, only a slight flinch as he fought down the urge of ingrained obedience to senior officers.

Enlisted man, Steve thought.

"What's your purpose here... sir?" the man asked in a quieter voice.

"Like I said, we're passing through," he replied. "We're from a group a week's journey to the south. I'm taking someone to the Highlands."

Still the man hesitated, keeping his weapon trained on Steve's chest.

"Look, we're friendly. We just want to be on our way," he tried again.

"Sorry, sir, can't let you do that," replied the soldier stiffly.

"On whose orders?" Steve invested the question with all the commissioned officer-like tone he could muster, seeing the man struggle with his sense of duty.

"Sir," he barked, "with respect, I'd ask you to remove your weapons and come with us voluntarily."

Steve sighed and slowly reached down to unclip the carbine. The soldier indicated for him to put it on the bonnet and add his sidearm and knife next to it.

"Please call your friend out, sir," he instructed politely. "Tell them to keep their hands up and move slow."

Steve called out to Emma, repeating the instructions. She came out and stood by his side. The soldier lowered his rifle a little but kept it at the ready. He assured them that they would be treated well as long as they showed no hostility, stuttering over his words, as he seemed a little transfixed with the attractive young woman who had emerged scared from the Land Rover.

They were searched and allowed to lower their hands before they walked with the soldier and two others through a gap in the deliberately piled-up vehicle barricade. They walked for about a mile before emerging through a treeline to see rows of large green tents lined up neatly against the wall of a big distribution warehouse. Activity flurried everywhere, and Steve lost count of the people but guessed he had seen almost a hundred of them.

Neither tried to engage the soldier in conversation, Emma preferring silence anyway and Steve electing to save his breath for the organ grinder.

They were walked into the huge hangar and into an outer office which previously would have belonged to the manager of this place. It now belonged to the commander of this group, with a heavy military theme running throughout. They sat and waited, even being offered coffee, until the door to the inner office opened and a clean-shaven young man smiled at them. He looked to be about mid-twenties, fit, and wearing a three-starred epaulette on the chest of his uniform.

"Captain Richards," he said in his soft Scottish accent, shaking their hands. "Formerly of the 51st Infantry, but now it seems I am officer commanding the 1st Battalion of Survivors." He smiled at his own joke, clearly having made it before on numerous occasions.

"Flight Lieutenant Steve Bennett, RAF," he replied, adding "retired" before he could be pressed instantly into active service by this enthusiastic young man.

The young officer's face lit up to find a fellow officer's mess buddy.

"Emma," she said quietly, taking the offered hand shyly.

"What were you flying?" he asked Steve, inviting them both to sit opposite his large desk covered in papers.

"Merlins mostly. Sea Kings to oil rigs most recently."

"Wonderful stuff," replied Captain Richards, brain working overtime behind his smiling eyes. "What brings you to our camp?" he asked.

"Your soldier frogmarched us here at gunpoint," Emma said, quiet but indignant.

"I can only apologise for that. I am truly sorry for the manner in which you were detained," he said, full of sincerity. "As you can imagine, there are some who don't play nicely with others." He shrugged, offering no further explanation.

"We've met our fair share," said Steve. "Tell us about what you have here, please."

Richards looked delighted, the perpetual mask of politeness and contentment on his face staying firmly in place. "We have almost one hundred and fifty survivors on the strength. We've established medical services and have sufficient stores stockpiled to sustain us for quite some time. We are looking to move in the future to an area we can easily occupy and grow supplies," he said, giving very little away. "What about yourselves?"

"Over a hundred of us, a week's journey south. Medical services and farms established. Well-armed and entrenched, as we've suffered some attacks," Steve said, embellishing the figures slightly, as he wasn't sure about their host just yet.

"Excellent!" Richards said as something flashed in his eyes. "Would you consider joining us?" he asked, taking them by surprise.

Steve answered carefully, not wanting to offend the brash man twenty years his junior. "We are well established and settled, but thanks. We've put a lot of effort into adapting our home, and I doubt anyone would want to leave."

Richards nodded but said nothing.

Steve was starting to trust him less.

"We seem to be in luck!" Richards said, changing the subject with startling suddenness. "We have a helicopter not far from here and now we have someone to fly it!"

Steve was taken back by the change of topic, and by reflex asked what it was.

"Chinook!" declared Richards with glee. "Bloody massive beast it is!"

Steve told him, regrettably, that he had never flown one. "They're not the easiest things to control; you'd need another pilot and crew to get one of those in the air. What about maintenance?" he asked, knowing that without significant skilled work, there was no way even a small craft would ever fly.

"I'm sure there are some manuals lying around," Richards said with arrogant dismissal of the problems facing his plans to get a helicopter in the air.

"It's not that easy, really–" Steve started, but was cut short with an irritated wave of Richards's hand.

"We'll discuss that later. Tell me why you're here," he ordered with a false smile.

Steve was wary. He didn't exactly trust what he was seeing here; it was too military, and Richards was deploying far too much effort in looking happy with life. He thought quickly but was unable to come up with a reason for their trip that didn't involve the whole truth. He looked at Emma, who met his gaze and shrugged. "Emma is a scientist and she wants to find a lab she knows to run some tests," he said simply.

Richards raised his eyebrows, but his smile stayed fixed in place. He leaned back in his chair and crossed his legs as he fiddled with a pen in his hand. "Tests?" he said lightly.

Emma shifted uncomfortably in her seat. "Yes. I want to check if the – if whatever it was – will mutate. There's a very small percentage of natural immunity, and a mutation could wipe us all out permanently. I need the lab because I know it's got the equipment I need to run the tests."

Steve tried to keep his face neutral as she smoothly lied next to him. He wanted to conjure up a story like that, as he didn't want to inflame the situation by mentioning biological warfare. Emma was providing exactly that, and it was coming out seamlessly. No doubt there was a lot of truth in the things she was saying, because it all sounded so realistic, but it was all news to Richards.

Richards listened intently, never once letting his mask slip as Emma made her explanations.

When she finished, Steve chimed in. "So we're hoping to get on our way as soon as possible."

Richards thought for a second and then sat forward with sudden movement. He stood, dropped the pen on his desk and invited them to tour his command with him. The invitation was less of a suggestion and more of an instruction, but Steve played along with the pretence of them being guests. They were led among the rows of tents, all neatly lined up in uniform rows. Richards struck Steve as a man who liked straight lines and obedience.

"Winter was hard on us," he explained as he paced in front of them. "Had to move everyone inside the hangar. It was a very unproductive time." He invested the word *unproductive* with scorn, as if the insult was a serious one. "Operations have gone well, though, on the whole. We're close to the point where we can send an advance party ahead to scout where we want to relocate." He stopped and turned to face Steve. "I'll not mess you around," he said intensely. "I want you to join us. You'll be given appropriate rank and have the pick of anyone you need to get me a bird in the air."

Steve was dumbfounded by the suddenness and directness of the man. He was also silent because he realised his first instinct wasn't to decline.

Richards turned to Emma before Steve could say a word. "And yourself too; we have a medical team, and your expertise will be valuable," he said.

Steve didn't know how to respond.

Before he had a chance, Richards let him off the hook. "You can go and do your thing first, obviously. I'd be pleased if you stayed with us tonight, and I'll provide an escort for you in the morning." He turned and walked on, giving no indication as to whether they should follow. They did, and Steve caught Emma looking at him with clear concern showing in her eyes. He thought the invitations and the offers of shelter and an escort weren't negotiable.

They were driven back to their Land Rover and followed their guide back to the camp via a smaller road. Steve locked everything but his sidearm away hidden in the vehicle and was conscious to keep the weapon tucked under his clothes. They settled in for an awkward night.

THE BODYGUARD

Their evening wasn't unpleasant. The people all went about their business in a subdued manner, and Steve was reminded of the times he had spent aboard large Navy ships. They were allowed to mix freely with the hundred or so people they could see in camp, and Emma found a fellow medical science type. They talked for a couple of hours about their theories and findings before Emma asked outright about Richards.

She was assured that it wasn't as bad as it seemed, but the way of life she described was basically military rule. They brought requests and suggestions to Richards, who had brought a handful of very well-equipped soldiers and lots of military hardware to the fold. It was a very tight ship they lived on, but they were protected, safe, and there was a plan.

They were given a tent with camp cots and shown where to get washed up after their evening meal, and Steve had relaxed sufficiently to not feel the need to keep the gun close.

Richards found them at breakfast and resumed his recruitment attempts.

"I trust you slept safely?" he asked, wearing his rigid smile.

Steve first thought it was a pretence, that Richards was more likely to force his will on people than respect an individual's choice. He was starting to realise that Richards was just a little awkward, and the smile was a bit of light social armour.

"Fine, thank you," Steve said. "I'd like to get on the road as soon as possible, though."

"I thought you would," Richards replied, and turned over his shoulder. "Andrews!" he called out.

Andrews came up and saluted before standing himself at ease. The slightly relaxed drill formalities spoke of a compromise for efficiency in an otherwise tight military-run camp. Andrews was about Steve's height and build but at least fifteen years his junior, and he was dressed in camouflage fatigues like Richards and carrying a sidearm on his right leg.

"All ready, sir," he said, nodding greetings to Steve and Emma.

"Andrews here will see you safely to your destination, not that I think you're incapable at all!" Richards said with genuine humour in his eyes.

They shook hands and promised to return with their answer on the way south. They followed Andrews out to the vehicles and saw a military Land Rover parked next to their own. Andrews put on a tactical webbing vest and loaded his rifle – a British Army issue SA80 with a scope. He didn't ask for the destination, just got behind the wheel and waited to follow. Steve had to wonder whether they were being guarded or protected.

Their journey resumed its normal pace as the weather closed in. This far north, they saw the damage that winter had caused to some of the roads; huge potholes carved chunks of the roads away. Normal cars would struggle to negotiate some of the bigger bits of damage, and Steve guessed that nothing short of an off-road vehicle would be able to travel within two years in some places.

They made a couple of stops; both times, Andrews was alert and capable, covering with his rifle and providing backup for Steve. When they finally stopped for the evening after a bumpy day's travel, Steve tried to get Andrews talking. He expected a brick wall of short answers and was surprised when he opened up. His name was Mitchell, he preferred Mitch, but the military habit of surnames had stuck.

He had never shed the bounds of Army service, despite the end of the world, and seemed fiercely loyal to Richards. He wasn't his captain; in fact, of the eight Army personnel there, only one was from Richards' unit originally. Mitch was one of six trained infantrymen who had been cobbled together to form the blades of Richards' survival camp.

"It's not that bad. We've had hard times and a few insurgent issues, but on the whole it's good," he said genuinely. "And when the plan comes together, we'll be stronger and hopefully pick up more people on the way. It's no small task to get this many people across country nowadays."

"True, it isn't," Steve agreed, sipping the coffee made on the camp stove. "Tell me about this helicopter."

"Airfield fifty miles from base. Chinook inside a hangar with some other fixed wings," Mitch replied.

"Any other helicopters?" Steve probed.

"None. The Chinook seems to be in good nick, though; when we found it, we locked the place down tight for winter. It's been sealed up ever since then, so should be well preserved."

"It'd need a full service; all the fluids would need changing," Steve said to nobody in particular, the thought of flying again clearly occupying his mind. "Tell me about the 'insurgents' you mentioned," he requested.

Mitch explained about the raids, attempts to steal their supplies by a group in the night. They had captured some of them and offered them a place at the table so they didn't have to steal. Some of them took the offered inclusion, others didn't. "It went on for a few months. I think in the end we killed enough of them to make it too much bother," he finished.

Their own story wasn't too dissimilar to how Richards's camp had grown, the main difference being that this group's core was military with an established hierarchy whereas their own was based more on a civilian government style. Both ways seemed to work. Richards had established a guard, trained capable civilians in weapon drills, fortified their position and sent out scouts just as they had and brought back more and more survivors. They hadn't encountered the same problems of having to liberate others from slavery – a story which intrigued Mitch mainly for the use of the big machine gun – and there seemed to be less resistance to their recruits here, perhaps due to the harsher terrain and the need for shelter taking over.

The more they spoke, the more Steve wanted to form some link with this group. Not that he wanted to join, but more that he felt that he could in some way help them. He tried to convince himself it was something other than the lure of getting behind the controls of an aircraft.

"There are other airfields in Scotland, you know..." Steve said.

THE FACILITY

It took them another two days to find it. They did so just as the light was starting to fade after they had covered the same patch of ground repeatedly looking for it. No handy signposts gave directions to the secret biological weapons development lab; that might have caused local residents to write to their MPs. Not that there were any local residents, as the land was bleak and empty.

The doors were unlocked and the ship-style airlock door swung open with a groan after the locking wheel was spun. No electricity – as they expected – so they cleared the place as best as they could with torches before finding the generator room deep underground. A jerrycan of diesel and some encouragement finally sparked it up with a series of threatening spluttering coughs. Slowly, the lights began to blink on and machines made whirring noises as they came to life. Steve and Mitch cleared the whole bunker, which was made up of ghostly labs and dusty glass doors.

They found no trace of anyone there, and assumed that they too had abandoned their haven when the power ran dry. Emma was lost in a rare moment of introspection, wondering if there were a huddle of decaying scientists in a building nearby, having escaped to certain death in excruciating pain. Her reverie was disturbed by the two armed men declaring that their temporary home was devoid of life other than their own. They set up in the living quarters, using their own sleeping bags and discarding the duvets belonging to the former inhabitants. Water was boiled, food was prepared and Emma formed a plan about the tests she wanted to run. Mitch gave her another sample of blood for her subject pool, and the lab was set to be reinvigorated the following day.

The following morning, Steve tried to offer his help, but after the third polite refusal, Emma allowed her exasperation to show.

"It will take me longer to explain the very basics of how to run a single test than it will to do it! Now please, let me work!" she snapped, softening her outburst with a smile and a drop of her shoulders. Truth was, she was very stressed. She knew where to start, but she didn't know where to end.

Steve got the hint and said that one of them would stand guard while the other scouted the local area.

Her analysis and comparison of blood samples between the immune and the now dead were the obvious initial places to look. She ran every kind of test she could: haemoglobin levels, white cell count, potassium levels, enzymes, platelets, and a dozen other checks. Each sample was carefully catalogued and the results were recorded in a large notebook as well as on her voice recorder.

After almost an entire day hunching over the worktop running the same tests repeatedly, she finally gave in to her aching back and growling stomach. There was probably another four days left just doing the basics before she even started work on the microscopic analysis of each sample. She left the lab to find Steve; they were going to be there maybe ten days, and the others needed to bring in supplies and more fuel. She found them both sitting in the communal area, decorated like an early nineties government canteen, and explained the timeframe to them.

Steve and Mitch looked at each other as though her declaration had touched upon a subject she wasn't aware of. Steve nodded to Mitch.

"I'll go," said the soldier, "first thing in the morning, and should be back in three days. You stay local and look for food and fuel."

Steve agreed, and he turned to Emma to explain.

"During my service, I spent some time up here; it's one of the reasons I volunteered to come, but I didn't want to get anyone's hopes up by saying why," he said, almost cautiously. "There is another Air Force base just over a hundred and fifty miles northeast. I'm hoping there is a smaller helicopter there that is preserved enough to get in the air. The Chinook is too big for me to fly alone, and the engineering required for it is extensive; plus, I've never even been in the cockpit of one, as flying them was always done by dedicated squadrons. Something smaller like a Sea King or a Puma or a Merlin would be much easier, and I've flown them all enough to know a bit about their engineering requirements. I want to get in the air again, if I can."

Emma understood. In her own way, she was enjoying what she was doing now; she had an expertise, and this was probably the last time she would get to use it. Steve was a pilot, and he felt like he'd lost the use of his legs since he'd last flown.

She raised no objection, and Mitch began preparing for a solo trip as they all pored over a large-scale map of the Highlands. Unlike their current location, the base would be well signposted, which would save a lot of searching. Steve planned to stockpile all the diesel he could find locally, having given Mitch his Land Rover for the journey, and Emma went back to her lab tests.

IMMINENT ARRIVALS

Dan relented and allowed the logistics crews to load enough baby equipment to last their growing colony for years. With all the powders and bottles and equipment, he reckoned they could raise kids for years, but still more was needed. Kate and her team wanted more and more medical equipment, and a return run to the hospital was suggested. Dan was not an advocate of ever visiting the hospital again, and was supported by Lexi as she absentmindedly rubbed at the thick scars on her chest.

Nobody had strayed far from home since Steve and Emma had left, and there was a slight air of anticipation about their expedition. Dan wondered why, as there could surely be no great revelations coming from the results. There could be no cure, nor was there anyone to be cured. They were what was left, and the only answers that could matter were to the questions of how and why.

On one of the morning tasking meetings, Joe and Lexi went out and Leah asked Dan for a minute of his time.

"I've figured it out," she said.

"What?" asked Dan, confused.

"The tyre-changing problem. You said I could go out alone if I could repair a flat tyre. I've figured it out."

Dan had completely forgotten about her driving assessment and felt bad, as she had been so disappointed that she couldn't lift the spare wheel down. After her recent performance, he trusted her abilities, but was still reluctant to let her out alone purely because he wanted to keep her safe. The tyre problem was a good excuse to hide behind until now.

"Tell me," he said, worrying that she had indeed surmounted the last remaining obstacle to her freedom.

"I've got a pump and some of that stuff you inject in so the puncture fixes itself. The pump runs off the car, so I can repair a flat and get home without having to take the wheel off," she said proudly.

As much as Dan wanted to find fault with it, she had presented a valid argument. He sighed with his head down, thinking.

"Dan?" she asked, concerned that she had got the answer wrong or had upset him. "What's wrong?"

"Nothing, kid," he said, giving in.

"It was nearly a year ago when I found you," he said wistfully. "You were a scared little girl, and now... Well, now you're just scary," he said, investing the last word with pride and admiration.

She beamed, pleased with the compliment.

"Let me run your idea past Neil, and I'll let you know," he finished.

"Today?" she pushed.

"Maybe. No promises."

She nodded and went back to looking busy over a map. His little girl was all grown up, in a way. He suddenly felt very sad that she was no longer vulnerable and weak, that she could look after herself despite her age. Modern society had made children stay dependent for so long; just a few hundred years ago, she would have been expected to be getting married soon, so was it really so bad that she was doing adult work now? She had adapted so quickly and efficiently to their new situation, and he couldn't hold her back much longer. Not without her resenting him. She'd trained intensively over the last nine months without taking a day off just to be the best she could be, and he couldn't deny that she was good.

With a heavy heart, he stood and left the house, Ash following at his heel without a command. Dan smoked as he walked slowly up to the farm, delaying the conversation as long as he could in good conscience. He found Neil with a hot drink and his feet up on the rear step of a Land Rover. Ash went straight to him and gave him an expectant stare until Neil's hand went to a pocket and came out with something for him.

Dan sat heavily and let out a long sigh.

Neil sipped his tea and guessed his friend's problems. "She asked you about the tyre pump, then, mate?"

"Yeah," Dan said with a tired smile, "she did."

"It's viable. I've got the stuff, and as long as she doesn't rip a wheel off, she should be fine. I've fitted a CB to her motor and was planning on repainting it black like yours," Neil said, way ahead of him as always. "Ready in two days."

"Thanks," Dan said. "Am I wrong? Is she ready?"

"She saved your arse, didn't she?" he replied. "Twice, as I recall!"

Dan smiled and leaned his head back. "She did, but I worry about her. She scares me a bit."

He meant it. Leah's abilities were impressive, but her cold attitude towards what she was becoming was his greatest concern. She had killed people. Killed people with the weapons he had given her and the training he had provided. She had calmly assessed situations and made ruthless decisions without hesitation, just as he did. The only difference was that he struggled with the decisions sometimes, whereas she seemed not to. He had had this discussion with Marie more than once. In her counselling sessions, Leah was very matter of fact about it, and the taking of a life was pure logic to her, necessary to protect the group, hence acceptable. She didn't have trouble sleeping, and she showed no signs of post-traumatic responses.

"In a way," Marie had told him, "she's better equipped to deal with this, as she has less to forget about from before. This is her life, and we are expecting her to still act like a child. She isn't, not anymore."

Dan had to accept it; she wasn't a little girl now. He had to let her go out into the hostile wasteland that was their home and trust that he had prepared her enough.

He left Neil with the project to finish Leah's vehicle and went to find Andrew to find out what stores were the next priority. A supply run for clothing and bedding was planned for three days' time.

SOLO MISSION

Leah's Land Rover was prepared and found sitting proudly with a new matt black paint job and a comedy set of pink dice hanging from the rearview mirror. Just after six in the morning, she shuffled in to Ops with her boots unlaced and a coffee in her hand, dumped her operational bag in the corner near the door and sat at the table.

A casually lazy salute was thrown Dan's way and followed by a sarcastic grunt of "boss".

Very similar to him: it was unwise to speak to her until the caffeine had soaked in.

He regarded her critically. She was thirteen, tall, and very leggy for her age, but her thin frame was wiry and strong. She moved like a predator, muscles taut like cables, but there was a kindness and compassion to her. Behind the façade lay an analytical mind capable of complex problem-solving, but her personality showed with her love for film quotes and sarcastic retorts. She was a product of their environment. An amalgamation of himself, Neil, Penny, Marie, Steve and others. It was time he trusted her.

"Supply run going out after breakfast," he said. "Make sure you've had something to eat."

"I know. I mapped the route," she said after blowing her drink. "That's yours, isn't it? Why do I have to eat now?"

"Because it's not mine," Dan said as he rose to his feet, followed by Ash. "It's yours," he finished as he slid the Defender keys across the table and walked out to hide his smile.

Leah sipped her drink and watched the keys slide to a halt just out of her reach, processing what Dan had said twice over, looking for the joke at her expense. She finally understood that he had just given her her own vehicle and her first command – she was going out, and not as anyone's sidekick. She was going solo.

Sipping her drink again, she watched the unmoving keys as it sunk in properly, then finished her drink in one large gulp and stood, stretching.

She walked outside and stood gazing at her own car, taking a slow lap around it to inspect the paintwork. The back section proudly showed a neat rank of puncture-repair bottles next to a large air pump, and a new CB radio was screwed tightly to the dash.

Still not quite believing the turn of events this early, she walked back inside and got herself a breakfast of thick toast and eggs. She washed down another coffee and stood, catching Jimmy's eye.

"Thirty minutes?" she said, trying to convey calm confidence and not let out the bursting excitement she was starting to feel.

Jimmy raised his cup in acknowledgement and she left the room. She went back to her own quarters after a visit to the bathroom and tied her hair up high in a ponytail. She looked at herself in the mirror, having a silent conversation where she reassured herself that she was ready. That she could do this. That she wasn't scared. She had been nagging to be let off the lead for weeks, and now she had been, the doubts hit her hard. She thought of going to find Dan and asking him to shadow her, but stopped herself. Drawing up to her full height, she held a long breath and let it out slowly.

"You can do this. Woman up!" she said quietly to herself before turning abruptly away and walking back downstairs. She strode confidently into Ops and donned her kit vest, pulling the Velcro tight with her diaphragm inflated. She checked the chamber of her Walther, screwed on the suppressor and flicked the under barrel light on and off to test it. She pressed her thumb down on the top of the two spare magazines she carried for the sidearm and secured the flap on top of the pouch. She retrieved her desert-dappled carbine and went through the familiar routine of checking the gun's action and the three spare magazines she carried for it before loading one into the breech and racking the bolt to seat a bullet into the chamber.

She applied the safety and slung the weapon over her body in completion of her ritual, then slowly walked towards the door, stopping only to write R5 in the "out" section of the chalkboard. She picked up her kit bag, always ready to go, and went to start up her vehicle. Rich stood leaning against the doorframe of the office and offered her a simple gesture as she walked by. She bumped his fist gently and left the house as he called, "Stay safe, Nikki."

Jimmy and his team of three others in their two small lorries were ready soon after, and all three vehicles met outside the front of the big house. This was Leah's first shot at taking the lead, and her mentor was nowhere in sight. Intentionally, she suspected.

"Morning, everyone," she started with confidence. "Dan's not on this run; I'm taking the lead instead." *Best get that out first*, she thought. She saw Jimmy smile, but one of the others pulled an obvious face at a teenager being in charge of them. She had to carry on before her confidence evaporated. "I'll lead the route, clear the target, and we should all be back safely this afternoon. None of us are new to this," she said, hoping that nobody pointed out that she'd never been out on her own before, "so let's get it done."

She nodded, and thankfully Jimmy filled the immediate silence by encouraging his teams to get moving. He shot her a sly wink and a warm, proud smile as he turned to his truck.

Thank God that went OK, she thought as she climbed behind the wheel. She would genuinely rather face armed attackers than have her confidence burst by people not wanting to go with her.

She peeled out, leading the convoy on a winding journey to their target. At about nine miles out, she picked up the mic and keyed it to call the house. Rich came back, acknowledging her transmission.

"Almost out of CB range. Will shout up when we are on the way back," she broadcast with partly faked confidence.

"Roger," said Rich. "Bring 'em home safe, Nikita."

The journey was uneventful, other than having to nudge one husk of a car out of the way to make space for the bigger vehicles. They arrived at their target and stopped in the car park of the small retail park. Leah got out and readied her weapon, and she nodded to Jimmy, who stood guard by the entrance with a shotgun. She checked the large sliding glass doors and found them locked. Conscious of the others watching her, she went to the large plate glass window and looked through before stepping back a few metres and flicking off the safety catch. She fired a single round into each corner from her suppressed carbine and watched in satisfaction as the glass shattered into a million pieces and cascaded down in a flow of small beads. She went through the wide gap, boots crunching on the shiny fragments, and set about clearing the warehouse-style showroom quickly and efficiently. It took her no more than five minutes to return and call the others inside.

"All clear," she announced. "Showroom and stockroom with no upstairs." She turned to Jimmy and told him she would clear the next building as they took what they wanted. Jimmy waved his team inside to collect beds and mattresses. She walked the short distance to the next building and repeated the entry process, taking longer to clear this time as there was a door leading to a narrow stairway and a series of small offices on a mezzanine floor. The wooden door with its keypad lock yielded to a single round from the carbine.

As she went back outside to see the others carrying the items they had come for, a noise at the edge of her hearing focused her attention. She couldn't place it, but something told her that it wasn't a natural noise, which set her senses on edge.

She ran to the nearest lorry and climbed on the wheel to reach the bonnet, from there hauling herself easily onto the roof of the cab to give her a commanding view of the area. She could see nothing, but the noise was still there, brought to her ears intermittently by the eddying breeze. Three minutes went by, then four and five, but still nothing came into view.

Jimmy saw her looking around like an alert sentry and asked her if everything was OK.

"Yeah. I can hear something in the distance, I think. How long?"

"Five minutes, then we'll hit next door for the clothing and bedding," he replied.

Leah stood watch for another fifteen minutes as the others moved into the next building and began to bring out armfuls of clothing and other things. A flash of movement at the extremity of her vision made her raise the weapon to look down the scope. Whatever it was that had moved was no longer there, but the noise was more pronounced now. She suspected that she had heard an engine, maybe more than one. She fought down the urge to call the others back and flee in panic.

Recalling what Dan had told her, she forced herself to stay calm. "Remember," he had told her, long before she had gained the experience to fully understand the true meaning, "we're probably the scariest things out there, so there's no need to panic."

She told herself this over and over, but the feeling of uneasy fear was growing in her belly like a rapid cancer. Jimmy came back and told her that they had filled one of the lorries but wanted to get the second one stocked from the next shop. She thought for a second before jumping down and pulling out a small pair of binoculars from her vest.

"Get up high and keep an eye out," she instructed. "There's definitely something moving around out there."

Jimmy nodded and she turned to open the third large commercial building. The sliding doors were unlocked, and with the help of the others, they were forced the rest of the way open. She repeated the clearing process, conscious not to rush the task and cause more problems. As she reached the extreme of the stock area, a single blast of a shotgun made her heart stop for a moment.

MAD MAX II

Leah turned on her heel and sprinted for the entrance to find the others milling about in mild panic. Her worst fears were alleviated when it became apparent that the shot was for attention and not aimed as a threat. To her left, she saw a handful of motorbikes slowly peeling into the car park and spreading out in a menacing pack. She dropped to one knee in the partial shelter of the entranceway and shouted at the others to get back in the vehicles. They had one shotgun per lorry, and Jimmy was standing on the bonnet of his truck with his legs planted widely. Leah scanned the approaching group through her optic and decided that they did not look friendly.

The bikes stopped in a line almost perfectly plotted for Leah to strafe the entire group. She stayed put where she was and slowly reloaded a full magazine into the carbine, flicking the fire selector to automatic. The bikes were all canted over onto their stands and one by one the engines were stopped to bring an echoing silence to their small battlefield.

Leah had no intention of letting her fears rule her, as otherwise she would have opened up on them immediately. She decided to see how it played out and gauge if they really were an enemy. She wasn't hopeful; their clothes were all ragged and they carried long knives and other cruel-looking weapons on their bikes. None of them wore a helmet, and the one who seemed to be the leader stepped forward and craned his neck up to Jimmy.

"What are you doing here?" he asked amicably enough, but a threat hung in his words.

"Shopping, mate. You?" Jimmy replied with his casual cockiness.

The biker held up his hands in mock defence. "No offence meant," he said without genuine meaning, "we're just being friendly."

Leah decided that he was not friendly. Not one bit. Jimmy got that impression too.

"Well, we're just leaving," Jimmy said without moving.

The biker boss tut-tutted and shook his head slowly. "No," he said slowly, "you're not. You're going to come back with us and be our 'guests'."

Leah had heard enough, and she reacted as three other decisions were made simultaneously. First, Jimmy swung the barrel of the Remington towards the bikers and brought the butt into his shoulder. As soon as he moved, four of the bikers reached into their jackets and pulled out weapons.

She didn't know who fired first.

"The point of any conflict is to kill them quicker than they can kill us."

Dan's words echoed in her mind afterwards, as she replayed what had happened. The bikers were still bunched up in a ragged line facing Jimmy as they drew. Leah had no time to differentiate between those aiming weapons; she just had to drop them quicker than they could drop Jimmy.

She fired five short bursts before she switched her aim to the last one. As she did so, her victim flew backwards, upper body bending unnaturally as he was thrown down by the huge impact of the shotgun. The conscious thought that he was already hit heavily did not enter her mind as she stitched a further line of bullets into him as he fell.

She rose to her feet, hands moving with much practised ease as she reloaded without looking. "COMING OUT," she yelled, not wanting Jimmy to panic and shoot her in case he was in shock. She went along the line of downed bikers. All dead with the exception of one trying to stem the thick flow of blood from the hole in his neck. He looked at her mutely, mouth opening and closing soundlessly, as he struggled to stop the arterial gush. His eyes went vacant in a second, and the hand relaxed to allow the last weak spurts to pour out with the rapidly decreasing pressure of his failing heart.

She turned away and looked to Jimmy.

"Are you OK?" she asked him.

He looked directly at her and gave a small nod, clearly horrified by the speed of what had just unfolded.

"Everyone else OK?" she shouted.

The other three emerged from the lorries unharmed. They were fine.

"Right, clear the last building quickly and let's get the hell out of here," she instructed them. She didn't know why she did that, but the focus of completing a task quickly brought them all back into the present, and they scurried away to comply.

Leah checked the bodies of the bikers she had ventilated, taking poor-quality and badly maintained weapons from them. She recovered a revolver, a semiautomatic pistol which she didn't recognise, and three sawn-off shotguns, leaving the large machetes and knives. The bike belonging to the leader had curious markings on the tank, and as she studied them closer, she was horrified.

Line after line of stick men and women were painted on with something that looked like Tippex; the realisation that this was the same as pilots in World War Two painting the outlines of planes they had shot down on their aircraft made her feel sick. These were bad people, and they deserved to die.

She thought about that for a second, changing her mind about the declaration she had just made to herself.

Her group deserve to live, and these people wanted to change that. That's why they were dead and she wasn't. She stood up, straightened herself, and shook off the brief violent encounter. She climbed back to her perch on the lorry and scanned for more danger as the others came out of the shop with the valuable supplies. With deft hands, she replenished her weapon with a full magazine without looking.

Leah was calm. She was shaking slightly, but she recognised the physical reaction to adrenaline and knew that it would fade soon. She sat on her right foot and rested the carbine on her raised left knee, slowly scanning the horizon and breathing slowly to return her body to normal.

She was calm, she was effective, and she was a leader.

She wouldn't recognise it herself, nor would she probably like to admit it, but she was also the most dangerous person in over fifty square miles.

AFTER-ACTION REPORT

Leah's convoy made it back in the afternoon. She had called home on the radio ten miles out, reporting a successful trip and a contact. Dan snatched the radio from Jack and asked for details, the nervous strain evident in his voice. Leah assured him that they were all fine and that she would give him a full report as soon as they were back.

She rolled down the drive and up to the front of the house to find Dan standing outside with Ash at his heel. The lorries peeled off to the store's shutters as she pulled up and reverse parked next to Dan's Discovery.

She readied herself to weather the storm of his questions, to account for the failings she had repeatedly cursed herself for on the return journey. She climbed down and saw him striding towards her with a pained look on his face. He didn't stop when he got to her, but carried on and threw his arms around her, picking her up easily. He held her tightly and breathed hard, relief washing over him. She fought out of his grip until he put her down.

"Air!" she gasped theatrically.

"Are you OK?" he asked, full of concern.

"I'm fine," she said. "Coffee?"

They went inside and Dan poured a coffee for them each. They sat at the table, where she began to strip down her carbine just as Rich came in. He took the weapon from her.

"I'll clean that. You two talk," he said kindly, and went to leave the room. Leah stopped him and threw him the keys to her Defender.

"Recovered some weapons on the front seat; they're in bad shape, I think," she said.

"From the beginning," Dan said, more calm now.

"Got there fine, cleared two buildings and I got up high to keep watch." She paused, sipping the hot liquid. "I thought I could hear noises – engine noises – but saw nothing. I cleared the third building after leaving a lookout and Jimmy fired a shot to get me back outside. Six men on motorbikes, not friendly." She stopped again, cooling the coffee by blowing over the lip of the cup.

"And?" Dan said, impatience creeping into his voice.

"I had the angle on them," she said, demonstrating the oblique lines with her hands, "and they drew on Jimmy after refusing to let us go. They didn't know I was there and they all went down. The others cleared the last building and we came home."

So matter of fact. So emotionless.

Dan didn't know whether to be impressed with her cool or worried that she was a psychopath. "Go on," he said.

"Bursts into each one. The last one I hit had taken one high in the chest from Jimmy's Remington. He had twenty-six stick men drawn on his bike. Some were women and some were smaller than the others…" She trailed off.

Dan knew exactly what that meant, and he was surprised to realise that Leah did too. "Any others?" he asked, getting back to business.

"No. I got back up high and saw nobody else. I put in two ambushes on the way home and didn't see a thing."

161

She had done well. Very *well*, he thought.

"You stayed after the contact to clear more supplies?" he asked, finally clicking with what she had said earlier.

"Yes. The others were in a panic and I thought that giving them a job to do would settle their nerves and they were less likely to crash on the way home."

Dan could see the logic in that, but even he wasn't sure if he had the guts to make that decision. The instinct to clear out of the area following a contact was so strong and ingrained that he knew his thought processes were different from hers on the subject. He regarded her as she loosened and removed her vest before picking up her coffee again.

Dan sighed. "OK, get a shower and see Marie please."

The lazy sketch of a salute again, and her personality broke through the curtain of his stress. She had been weighed and measured, and she had not been found wanting.

She transferred her Walther to the hip holster she wore when off duty and stowed the rest of her gear as Dan drank his coffee before she left to clean up.

Hearing her leave, Rich emerged from Dan's old bedroom and came to sit with him.

"Well?" he asked.

Dan sighed again and looked to the ceiling, tilting his head back and rubbing his face. "She took out six armed men who, I reckon, were quite accustomed to violence. You tell me."

"That's our girl," Rich said, smiling.

"How do you feel about it now?" Marie asked, leaning forward slightly in her chair.

Leah shrugged. "Fine. I had to do it or the five of us would probably be dead by now and the supplies wouldn't be here," she replied. She wanted to say that she wasn't uncaring about it; she knew she had killed people, which was fundamentally wrong, but it was either them or her. There was no simpler way to explain it. "If they were friendly, I wouldn't have done it, you know that, right?" she asked Marie, mimicking her posture in the chair.

"Yes, I know that," Marie answered with a soft smile. "I just want to be sure that you know that."

"Well, yeah. Obviously. I know you all think I'm cold about it, but it's us or them – I chose us. Honestly, I think Jimmy needs you more than I do right now."

"OK, but promise me you'll come to me to talk about any feelings you have about it?" Marie said.

"I promise. I'm fine about it; it's just one of those things that happens now."

Leah helped herself to another biscuit as she got up to leave. She had skipped the shower and decided on going for a run. She put on shorts and a T-shirt, tying the waistband tight to hold the holstered Walther inside by the small of her back. She laced her trainers tight and went back downstairs, poking her head into Ops, where Dan was still sitting.

"That dog of yours need a run?" she asked.

"Yes," Dan replied. "He keeps farting, and it smells like a dead badger; by all means take him!" He never minded letting Ash go with her, as he felt better that she had backup even though she wouldn't leave the immediate area.

"You carrying?" he asked as she patted her legs for Ash's attention.

In response, she turned and showed him her back without a word. Dan nodded at her.

"Go on then, stinky," he said as his dog went to her with his tail wagging. "And you, Ash," he finished, as she knew he would say.

Leah ran across the fields to the gardens, Ash loping by her side but still looking up at her expectantly. She stopped at the road and looked both ways, surprising herself at the ridiculous gesture deeply ingrained into her mind.

After a mile, she had to stop and wait for his ridiculous ritual of sniffing desperately before returning to the first spot to deliver his payload. He scratched all four feet backwards in turn, digging at the ground before bounding after her with renewed energy at his immediate weight loss. She set a brisk pace, making her breathe hard as she ran. Ash kept up effortlessly, still hoping for a treat of some description.

She stopped after a few miles of cross-country circuits to catch her breath. She worried herself a little bit if she was honest; why wasn't she affected by killing people? Would everyone be happier if she burst into tears and wept for the loss of life at her hands?

No, she decided. She wouldn't fake emotions just for other people to feel happier, and if she was to take control in the future, then she must be strong. That, she knew, she wasn't faking. She was strong. She wasn't upset about killing those men, but then again she didn't enjoy it either. It was a task. A job. It needed doing and she did it.

Which was exactly what she would always do to keep these people safe.

She started to run again. Taking a long route back to the house, she set a faster pace, pushing herself.

EAT, SLEEP, TEST, REPEAT

Emma's eyes were dry. The air-conditioned atmosphere in the bunker was something that she had forgotten, but now the memory of how it made her feel ill flooded back. She was tired; she needed fresh air and sunlight.

She made herself a drink and took it outside into the blustery Scottish summer evening. The wind blew hard against her, making her wrap the fleece around her body. She let the cool air blow away the claustrophobia. So far, she had tested almost every blood sample she had. Other than finding some unrelated differences – likely congenital issues which had nothing to do with the virus or whatever it was – there was no difference. She had yet to isolate exactly what it was, but she found nothing in the samples of those who had died in front of her.

As she stood and enjoyed the breeze, the undeniable realisation became more and more clear. There had to be something, otherwise everyone would still be alive and life would be normal. Logically then, the fact that each sample showed no difference must mean that each sample was relatively the same. That meant that every sample of blood she had tested was exposed to the same infection.

"We all have it," she said out loud to herself.

Nobody answered, as she knew they wouldn't. She lacked the knowledge or the equipment to test DNA, so couldn't even begin to isolate any possible reasons why the survivors were immune.

She had drawn a blank. As far as she could tell, everyone was exposed to "it," but some just survived where most others didn't. Exasperated, she threw the remaining half of her drink into the grass and went back inside. She wandered into the lab and decided to pack up her research, as there was nothing new she could learn. As she moved her large notebook, she saw a scribbled note on a desk pad by a computer terminal. It read "H_FLE181. Password: SC13nceGEek1973. Desktop file 'TOP SECRET'."

Emma stared at the note, not believing that she hadn't seen it before. She carefully moved her bundle of notes to the side and settled in front of the computer terminal. She pressed the power button and watched patiently as the lights and sounds started up. Eventually she was faced with a login screen. She selected the correct user and carefully replicated the password.

The small folder icon bore the words "TOP SECRET" underneath, and she double-clicked it.

WHIRLYBIRDS

Mitch made good time getting to the base. It took him far longer to winch every hangar open by hand. The huge doors in the sunken, grass-covered tunnels inched open with every muscle-burning effort, eventually allowing him enough space to get inside and search. The dried bodies of a couple of RAF police still sat in their office, their sentry duty set to last until their bones corroded away to dust.

The first hangar was empty. The second housed a massive C-130 transport plane. He found what he wanted in the third hangar as his torch beam illuminated the tail rotors of an RAF Merlin. The rear ramp was down and he walked up it, boots clanging with a metallic sound as he went. It seemed well preserved and undamaged. He had been a passenger on helicopters in the past, even jumped out of a plane similar to the behemoth parked next door, but had never been in the cockpit of an aircraft.

He was in awe of all the dials, buttons, switches and gauges. He couldn't imagine ever learning what they all did, but then he was always happy with his place in life. His place had always been to sit in the back and wake up when they told him to get out. With his limited knowledge and Steve's instructions, Mitch decided that this was exactly what they wanted.

He looked for the other things on the list he had been given, finding the aviation fuel stores and the engineering workshop. Manuals lined a large bookcase in large ring binders. He decided to search the rest of the buildings and stay the night before making an early start and hopefully getting back within the day.

A small arms locker was located in a guardroom, and Mitch took the semiautomatic pistols along with the spare ammunition. He made himself a bed in the most comfortable place – the mess room with the large settees – and ate a dinner of the cold contents of the tins he carried. He was never one for comfort even before this turn of events, having joined the Army as a teenager and spent his whole life living in cold and uncomfortable conditions. He lay back and dreamed of riding around in the back of a helicopter again.

WHY MESS WITH THINGS YOU DON'T UNDERSTAND?

Emma read the notes on the Word document which was first in the list. The file held numerous files and videos, each one making her world less and less believable.

The documented notes on the file referenced a Japanese science team visiting the Arctic Circle. A US-government-run site had a science team drilling into the ice, nominally as an archaeological project. Science teams from all over the world visited under the "protection" of the American Special Forces teams permanently in place.

Emma had been to a number of government-run science projects, and every one, without fail, had been a weapons-testing project: accelerant for rocket fuel; material bonding for stealth planes and satellite technology; and, in her field of virology, bioweapons research.

This ice drilling went down so deep that it preceded the ice age and went back millions of years, even past the dinosaurs' extinction event. It wasn't enough to stop there; they had already gathered more data and samples and fossils than they could analyse, but they still had to drill further.

The first few videos showed scientists documenting their finds and discussing theories. They were all wearing protective suits, and the footage looked to be Go-Pro style. She held her breath as she watched, genuinely terrified of what could be down there.

She clicked through three videos of similar scenes, two of which were in foreign languages she didn't recognise. The next document was a lab report analysis of biological tissue remains. The report showed the carbon dating of the sample making it almost seventy million years old.

This was huge. All that remained of this time were fossilised remains, not actual biological tissue. The years she had wasted reading science fiction overloaded her brain with wild ideas; the consequences of handling biological matter from that long ago were enormous. Without reading further, she was sure that this had to have something to do with the phenomenon causing most of the population to die.

She slumped in her chair, mouth open, and staring at nothing. She didn't see or hear Steve come in, and when he spoke, she screamed in fright.

"Sorry," he said, chuckling, "I didn't mean to startle you."

Emma opened and closed her mouth to answer, but no words came out.

"What's wrong?" asked Steve, instantly losing the humour he had found in her initial reaction. "What have you found?"

Emma recovered her voice. "They found something under the ice. Seventy million years old. I think that's what killed everyone." She turned to stare at him.

"Show me," he said.

Emma quickly explained what was in the documents she had read and showed the videos to him. She went on to the report and had to decipher it for him. "They found biological tissue," she said. "Preserved. Frozen under the ice from before the event that led to the extinction of the dinosaurs."

He didn't see the relevance, which frustrated her. It had felt like years since she had been the only scientist in the room.

"It would be like introducing viral meningitis to medieval times; humans wouldn't be prepared to cope with whatever they've found in there – there's no way of knowing if it was dangerous to us!"

Steve understood. "How could they be so reckless?" he asked, astonished.

"They probably thought they were smarter than nature. Clever people have a way of being very stupid sometimes."

The next two videos made the discovery clear. A high-definition setup in a lab showed a team of scientists working around a small bench. They were speaking Japanese, and despite the face masks, Emma could tell they were excited. They were thawing out the sample carefully and running various tests on it as they went. When the ice had been thawed, Emma saw what it was.

A plant. Dark green stem and leaves and a large purple petal remained around the stoma.

The video ran on for another thirty minutes. Neither of them moved nor spoke, despite not understanding what any of the scientists were saying. The date in the lower left-hand side showed just over a year ago.

The next file was an email. It had an undecipherable address but was from a government server.

```
BIO SITE STAFF ONLY - CABINET NOT INFORMED.
Japanese gov tests on prehistoric bio-matter have
caused fatal side effects. Unknown source but
possibly pollen from flowering fauna.
Initiate lockdown immediately. Cabinet not
informed to date; lockdown procedures initiated.
Public not informed. No sign of hazard reaching
UK. Await instructions.
```

No signature. No other information. The time stamp on the email was about three hours before she had been swept away to her own bunker. They sat in silence for a while.

"Just so I understand this," Steve said slowly, "explain to me what I just learned."

Emma took a long breath and let it out slowly. "Scientists found a seventy-million-year-old plant preserved in the ice from the cretaceous period. They thawed it out and the pollen caused them to be ill," she said carefully. "After that, I can only theorise."

"Please do," Steve said quietly.

Emma chewed her lip for a second, running the idea through her head to check for flaws before she spoke. "The pollen caused a reaction. That reaction must have become viral, otherwise the pollen could not have swept over the planet. Airborne viral reaction, average fifteen hours for symptoms to show, death follows within forty-eight. We've been wiped out by a plant that shouldn't be on the planet anymore."

Both sat there and absorbed the information.

"So why are we alive?" she said, picking the words from Steve's mind.

"Exactly," he said.

"Can't help you there," she said, moving for the first time in minutes. "We've all got it."

Steve looked shocked.

"I think," Emma added lamely.

"You think?" Steve said with a frown.

"Yes. There are no obvious differences between the blood results. I can't say why we survived, but there's no possible way we haven't been exposed to it."

Steve rubbed his face with both hands. He got up to leave, telling her he needed some time to think it over.

She returned to the computer after he walked out, almost punch-drunk, and started looking at the files again from the beginning.

How stupid.

How stupid and arrogant and foolish.

The curiosity of human nature seemed to have condemned its own existence.

ROYAL DECREE

Patrick was not happy. He had been shamed, outclassed and sent packing. He brooded over taking revenge on that arrogant bastard and his evil-tongued bitch.

Obviously, he had no intention of getting his own hands dirty. He had his boys to do that. This wasn't the medieval era; kings weren't expected to don shining armour and ride at the very head of the vanguard anymore.

No, he would be clever about it. Any attack on their base would likely result in a mild case of death with a side of brutal retaliation, so he would have to find another way.

For over a week now, his boys had been searching for a base closer to the prison, somewhere they could keep an eye on their comings and goings and report back. This had worked wonders, and already he had built a picture of what their routine was. The plan was forming in his head nicely, and he was close to a formal declaration of war. His boys knew it was coming. The fact that their efforts to find more weapons and vehicles had doubled was a clear indication.

Patrick wanted to return the shaming on Dan, and he intended to bleed him slowly.

"Gather round, my boys," he bellowed as he hauled himself to his feet. "The time has come," he said confidently, looking at the faces of the assembling ragtag army. "I'm sick of scratching a living, and I know you are too." He waited for agreement. It wasn't coming, not yet. He had to whip them up. "There's a nice place over the border, and I want it. I want it for us. I want their supplies."

A murmur of agreement from the assembled faces.

"I want their warm beds and their electricity."

Louder now.

"I want their hot water and their guns," he said, voice rising with every word.

A cheer began.

"I want their farm… AND I WANT THEIR WOMEN!"

Arms were raised. The cheer became a shout and the shout became a chant.

"PA-TRICK, PA-TRICK, PA-TRICK, PA-TRICK…"

Satisfied, the overweight man sat down and smiled, accepting the praise with a regal wave of his hand. The time was now. He would move his best force up and take the bastard.

Three days later, they moved their temporary camp to within five miles of the prison. It was done carefully, not in convoy so as to avoid detection. Their ambush plan was set.

COMPLACENCY

Leah was on duty in Ops and had the coffee ready for after breakfast when the others gathered.

Steve's absence was starting to be noticed; nearly two weeks without him had left a gap in the team makeup. Also, the workload was harder on everyone, even now with Leah not wearing her armbands as Rich joked.

Rich had started taking all the night duties to relieve the pressure; he said he never slept much anyway and took about five hours over lunch to refresh himself. He still looked awake in the briefing now.

"What have we got then, kid?" Dan asked, receiving an annoyed look in return. He made a mental note to treat her more like an adult in front of people.

"Lexi, protection for scavenging team." She slid the map around to show Lexi the location.

"Dan and Joe, recce farmland for any animals and other stuff. Here's a list of what Chris and Ewan want." She passed them both a piece of paper.

"Dan, you're going south, and Joe north."

Both nodded.

"I'm stuck here" – a hint of petulance crept in before she got a hold of herself – "and Rich will do the afternoon rounds to the farm and gardens."

"OK," said Dan, "let's do it."

Rich passed their weapons out one by one and they all went through their familiar routine of gearing up.

Within half an hour, they were all gone. Leah sat back in the office and turned the music up a bit, conscious not to drown out any sound that could come from the CB radio.

Joe made his way on the familiar roads, half asleep as he always was this early. He had never been a morning person.

Perhaps the fog on his brain made him utterly fail to see the danger. Perhaps he was doing a job that he wasn't experienced enough for. Not trained well enough. Maybe he was just having a slow day.

If he had been switched on, he would have realised there was something so horribly wrong with the vehicle blocking the road.

If he had been switched on, he would have stood off and called Dan back, or made contact with Leah, or done something, anything other than what he did.

Lazily, he drove up to within a few feet of the wreck and got out. As he bent to unhook the heavy rope from the front bumper, he heard a scrape on the concrete from behind him. He froze, suddenly aware of his vulnerability. He only carried the Glock on his leg; the M4 sat uselessly in the cab of his Defender. He spun, drawing the weapon as he moved.

Nothing. He stood motionless in a half-crouch with the gun held in both hands out in front of him. Slowly, he calmed and stood up, sliding the gun home in the holster.

He never saw the baseball bat swing from behind him. The sickening *crack* as it hit him full in the back of the head echoed between the derelict cars over the sound of his diesel engine idling.

He fell to the floor like a bag of sand, lights out.

SCOTLAND, IT'S BEEN FUN

Mitch got back just as the sun was starting to sink. He was excited about finding the preserved helicopter, and was careful to seal the hangar to keep it that way.

He returned to find the mood low. Steve was sitting quietly on a chair outside in a T-shirt, carbine resting across his knees.

"What's up?" Mitch asked, picking up on the total lack of excitement at his return.

Steve sighed and stood, throwing away the dregs of his coffee. "Emma's got to the bottom of it," he said tiredly. "I'll let her explain."

They sat down together in the lounge area and Emma gave a simple explanation. Mitch was unfazed; typically, with a soldier's mentality, he reckoned that anything not directly affecting him in the immediate future wasn't a concern.

Emma had transferred all the files to her laptop, and they planned to get back on the road the following morning.

They set off early, and as they drove south retracing their steps, she was quiet again. She couldn't get the possibilities out of her head about the effects of the virus on those who were immune. Her mind raced, but she didn't have the knowledge or the equipment to find out; she hated not knowing the answers to things, which was exactly why she had become a scientist.

It took them three uneventful days to get back to Richards' camp, and Mitch led them through the roadblocks without challenge. A familiar feeling of claustrophobia descended on Steve; he found that he much preferred the freedom granted by Dan to the thought of returning to military service.

Richards was his usual unconvincingly exuberant self and listened intently to the results of their trip. They agreed not to hide their findings from him, as the information was mostly irrelevant now.

After they ate, Richards asked Steve for a private word. He led him to his office, past the two armed sentries as they returned the salutes, and produced a bottle of Chivas and two crystal tumblers from the bottom drawer of his desk.

Steve recognised the officer-to-officer approach; he had seen it so many times in the past that it had no effect on him. It hadn't for years, not since he was a young man proud to be in exalted company.

"So, Andrews tells me he's found a bird you can fly," he said with veiled excitement. He seemed desperate to extend his military might to the skies.

"Maybe," replied Steve in an equally languid style as he leaned back and sipped the fiery drink. "It all depends on how many good engineers you have."

"Five. All experienced. They should be able to use the manuals to fill in the gaps in their knowledge, and of course your experience will be wholly necessary." The way Richards said it made his cooperation a foregone conclusion.

Steve had to tread carefully; he didn't want his liberty removed, which was clearly in Richards's power. "Absolutely," he said, taking another drink to give himself time to think. "I'll get back as soon as

I've taken Emma home and head up there with the engineering team. Hopefully I can get in the air again." He finished with a disarming smile and raised the glass in toast.

Richards reciprocated the gesture. He was quite ready to call the two briefed sentries in to detain and disarm this valuable man, but better to encourage his love for flying than force him into the role. Still, he could not afford to let him out of his sight. "Very well," he said, "let's talk in the morning." He drained his glass and stood, dismissing Steve.

He maintained his smile right up until Steve's footsteps echoed into silence before summoning the two soldiers outside. He sat and crossed his legs as they entered and stood to attention, salutes quivering.

"Keep watch on them all night; I don't want them leaving." He looked directly in their eyes to make the point clear. "Is that understood?"

"Yes, sir," they chorused before turning to their left and leaving.

Richards poured himself another measure and leaned back in his chair.

Steve went to find Emma. He was worried because he fully expected to have his weapons taken from him and the keys to his Defender seized, but the implication of freedom concerned him greatly. He found her lying on her camp cot, staring at the ceiling of the tent. He walked in and knelt next to her, making her recoil slightly at the encroachment into her space.

"I don't think they're planning on letting us go," he whispered close to her ear.

Her eyes showed panic and her breathing became rapid as the fear rose in her chest. She retained the wherewithal to keep her voice to a whisper in response.

"What do we do?" she asked in terror.

"I need to get you out of here. Do you think you can find your way back?"

Her eyes widened as she processed what he was saying.

"What about you?" she hissed, making him raise his hands in a calming gesture.

"It's really me they want; I want you to get home and tell them where I am," he said, sure that they would pursue them if he went too.

She thought on that for a minute, wondering how he could possibly be rescued. He seemed to read her thoughts as he cut off the next question.

"That helicopter should fly. As soon as it's in the air, I'll be flying it straight home; it'll only take me a few hours or so," he said, the plan forming in his head. He pushed away the thoughts of what he would do if he couldn't get airborne.

"OK," she said, "what do I need to do?"

Steve whispered his instructions of how she could get out of the complex. The benefit of her analytical mind meant that she had clear memories of the way out.

"All you have to do is head south; make as much progress as you can and only stop when you need to. When you do stop, you hide."

"I don't know how to find the prison, though!" she whispered with the expression of a worried but brave child.

"All you have to do is get within twenty miles of home and use the radio. Tell them where you are and they can come and find you," he said, sure that this was the only way either of them would get away.

"When do we do it?" she asked.

"I'm not sure yet. Soon, though. Be ready."

She nodded and quietly put her belongings back in her bag. He gave her the keys and asked her where her gun was. She had left it in the glove compartment.

Steve racked his brain. He was sure they would let her go if he could only get her outside the compound; he was the real prize. He decided to act normal and fill the time by looking for Mitch.

As he emerged from the tent and stood upright, one of the sentries from Richards's office ducked his head out of sight. It had already started, then. Steve stood tall and sauntered with confidence directly towards where the sentry had been. He rounded the corner and almost bumped into him.

Steve's feigned surprise was hopefully taken as genuine as he apologised and walked off towards the mess hall. Mitch was there, showered and changed and tucking into a plate of something that looked fairly undesirable.

Steve sat opposite him and chatted amiably. Steve was unsure if he should bring him into his confidence; certainly if he helped, then it would make Emma's chances of escape much better. They chatted generally as Steve tried to gauge the risk in telling him.

"You seem a little distant," Mitch said, fishing.

"Yeah. Long journey, you know?" Steve answered vaguely.

Mitch finished his mouthful and put down the fork he was using to shovel the food into his mouth. He leaned forward and spoke softly. "This got anything to do with your two shadows?" he muttered.

Steve gave a hint of a smile to fake some confidence. "Two? I'd only clocked the one," he said truthfully.

"Let me guess," Mitch went on, barely moving his mouth. "You don't think you're going to be allowed to leave tomorrow, do you?"

"No," he replied after a thoughtful pause, deadly serious.

"So why come to me?" Mitch asked, looking him straight in the eye.

Steve had to show his hand or fold; there was no other way. "I'll stay, but I need Emma out," he said after a long pause, hoping Mitch wouldn't burn him.

The soldier leaned back and picked at his teeth before draining his mug and burping behind his hand. "Tricky, that," he said cryptically.

The two men regarded each other for a while. Mitch didn't need to point out the position of power he was in, that he could just tell the soldiers watching Steve that he was planning an escape.

"I've had no orders," he said.

Steve didn't know what he meant by that yet, so he kept quiet.

"So I wouldn't be breaking any orders by giving you some help, would I?" He smiled and stood, collecting up his tray. He leaned over and slapped Steve on the shoulder with the smile still stuck in place, muttering like a ventriloquist as he did. "Her tent. Ten minutes. Be ready."

He left and Steve stood, not quite believing or trusting that he had a better chance of getting her out.

WHERE'S JOE?

Lexi's supply run went smoothly, getting back without incident and with a full lorry. The supply situation was healthy with fresh meat, salad and vegetables arriving daily. Neil ventured out with them to fill his tanker, and he peeled off to fill the reserve tank on the farm, as it was the most commonly used.

Dan had scouted a number of places where stray livestock had survived and could be added to their menagerie, and hadn't seen a single person since leaving the house that morning. All the locations were marked on the map, and Ewan could happily spend the next week rounding up more livestock and recovering the few machines they had asked the Rangers to look out for.

Leah was still in a slight mood but was hiding behind efficiency by taking detailed accounts of the trips; it was unnecessary, really, but thoroughness wasn't to be discouraged.

"What about Joe?" Dan asked her.

"Not back yet," she fired back without looking up from her work.

Dan frowned. He checked his watch and couldn't think why Joe would have been out this long, as his route was shorter than his own. He must have found something useful. He tried to push the feeling of impending doom away but couldn't. He walked to the radio and called into the mic.

No response.

He tried again, louder and with more authority, as though that would force the signal out further.

Still nothing.

He checked his watch again, forgetting that less than a minute had elapsed since his last look. There were still four or five hours left before darkness.

His decision was easily made. He snatched up his bag and turned to Leah. "Shotgun?" he asked her.

She looked up at him, quickly figuring out that he wasn't asking for a shotgun but wanted her to ride with him. She put down her pen and stood, walking out of the office and back in after a couple of seconds, carrying her M4 as she stooped to pick up her bag.

"Let's go," she said, whistling for Ash as she turned. Ash stopped panting and looked up at Dan.

"Go on then," he said, releasing the dog to lope out after the girl.

They drove north, following roads they had both travelled many times. They passed the small, now empty shop where she had cleared her first building with a loaded weapon. That seemed like so long ago.

After a few more miles, Dan slowed as they headed towards a small cluster of vehicles. He had personally cleared the way sufficiently to get their lorries through almost a year ago. He wasn't sure, but something just didn't seem right.

"Stay," he said as he opened his door. "You too, Ash."

"Hilarious," she said as she opened the large electric sunroof and stood on the seat to scan with her carbine.

Dan walked slowly forwards, seeing clearly what was wrong. A small car, once red and now a grimy off-pink colour, was facing the wrong way. There were clear gouge marks in the road surface where the long-ago perished tyres had failed to prevent the pitted wheels from leaving fresh scars in the tarmac.

Dan froze like a mannequin for a moment, then bent down.

Leah watched on as Ash whined and fidgeted to see his master all of forty metres away without him. She watched him bend down, then stand abruptly and raise his weapon. She flicked off her safety and bent to the scope, scanning desperately for the unseen threat. He backed away, returning to the Discovery, head turning different ways as he stepped carefully.

Leah kept her eye to the scope, lifting her head intermittently to get the wider picture. Dan reached the driver's door and got in.

"What is it?" she asked, still searching.

"Blood," Dan said, selecting reverse and turning his head to look past the curious dog on the back seat.

Leah braced herself and maintained her position until Dan turned a wide half-circle, selected drive, and accelerated away. She flicked on the safety catch and held the gun vertically as she slid back down into the passenger's seat to stare at him.

"The car had been moved. It was an ambush," he said, looking straight ahead.

Leah thought for a second, absorbing the news before her logical brain calculated the appropriate response. She reached for the CB but stopped herself just as Dan opened his mouth to deny her using it.

"They've got his Defender, and his radio," she said aloud, figuring it out.

"Yeah," he replied, wondering with fear who "they" were.

He drove them fast back to the house, stopping at the gardens and the farm to summon everyone back to the safety of the house.

The sun was sinking when he called the Rangers and the council members to cram into Ops. A worried buzz of excitement had spread among their group. Dan stopped that dead in its tracks with his first words.

"Joe's been captured. They have his weapons and his vehicle, so NO CB RADIO USE AT ALL." He let that sink in. "I don't know how and I don't know who, but there was a deliberate blockage on the road – here," he said as he quickly scanned and jabbed his finger at the site on the large map on the wall.

People craned to see the location, like it made a difference to them.

"There was blood on the road," he finished.

"Who took him?" Marie asked over the stunned silence in the small room.

"I don't know. Possibility that it's someone we've already encountered is slim; the group who attacked us are all dead, the ones we attacked I highly doubt could have found us, and the bikers we met took too much automatic fire to risk this, if there are even any of them left. This was carefully planned. Someone targeted us."

As soon as he said those words aloud, he met Marie's eyes and the flash of understanding between them made him feel cold in his stomach. She raised an eyebrow in silent question, looking for corroboration of their joint epiphany.

"The Welsh," he said to the group, receiving more silence in return. "They see it that we attacked them, then they followed us and found our home. You all know what they wanted with their little farcical visit, and we sent them away with a promise to kill them if they came back."

Again, nobody spoke for a few seconds. Rich cleared his throat. "Regardless of who it was, what do we do about it?" he asked.

"We find them and we get Joe back. We can bargain with them, give them a few weapons if needs be just to get them to leave," said Kate.

"That won't work," Leah said quietly. She stood a little taller and raised her voice in volume and confidence. "It won't work because they don't want to force a deal. Look at what they did; they picked off a single Ranger and now they have weapons and can listen to our radios. That's strategic. They are cutting the head off the snake."

It was Dan's turn to stare in stunned silence. Thirteen years old and wiser than most in the room in some ways. He couldn't fault her logic, as always.

"I think she's right," Lexi chimed in. "It's the only way to take over this place, to take out the few fighters and force obedience on the rest. We've proven what happens to anyone attacking in force before," she added, like any of them had forgotten the murderously one-sided battle.

"Options," Dan said, a familiar question to his Rangers, but the civilian contingent in the room stuttered as though something profound was expected of them each.

"Make contact on the radio, open a dialogue," said Neil, more subdued than ever.

"Set up OPs in each direction under darkness," said Rich, suggesting that two of them hide and observe the roads for any sign of the unseen besieging force.

"I'm in favour of negotiating," said Andrew, ever acquiescent.

"I'm in favour of finding every last one of them and putting them against the wall," spat Jimmy vehemently. It was unlike him to show anger, which betrayed just how scared he was.

As Dan was considering action over inaction, assault over negotiation, the radio crackled into life.

"Are you listening, boyo?" said the smug voice.

PAROLE

Steve had to hope that Mitch wouldn't turn him in. He only had the Sig on his chest and three magazines, so any kind of gunfight was likely to end quickly with him sporting some very unfashionable holes in his torso. He had to try and distract the soldiers enough so that Emma could slip away in their Defender and get far enough south to hide from them.

Hopefully he could convince Richards that she wasn't worth pursuing, that he was the prize and he would stay to fly his helicopter as long as they let the girl go. He considered asking this instead of planning her escape, but the risk of refusal and her imprisonment was too high.

He had slipped through the lines of tents to whisper to Emma through the canvas. Twice he bumped into people, pretending on impulse that he had been drinking. It worked, so he kept up the act and looked for the sentry who was trying to casually dog his steps around the camp.

"I want to see Richards. Take me to him." He invested the instructions with as much officer-like privilege as he could, seeing the ingrained obedience tug at the man.

"The captain," he said stiffly, "is not to be disturbed in the evenings."

"Rubbish, man," he snorted at him, "and you will call me 'sir'," he said as he walked past him, brushing his shoulder and striding towards Richards's office with the sentry scurrying after him. He didn't know where the other one was, but hopefully causing a commotion would bring him out to support his fellow soldier.

It worked. He was effectively blocked at the doors inside the large hangar and was attracting a bit of a crowd. The soldiers tried the respectful route, calling him 'sir' and gently asking him to keep his voice down, but soon they had to resort to shouting over him as he completely ignored them. That raised the noise level sufficiently to draw out Richards, who demanded to know what all the commotion was.

Emma heard the shouting and knew she had to move. The Land Rover was big and unfamiliar, and she didn't look forward to having to drive it, but it was her only way out and she had no desire whatsoever to stay here. She stole out of the tent as quietly as she could, keeping to the shadows and making for the car park area. She reached the car and hit the fob to unlock it; the six orange flashing bulbs which would have lit the area like a muzzle flash thankfully didn't illuminate due to the fact that all six had been removed to maintain the low profile they enjoyed. The electrical sound of the locks whirring and the click as the driver's door opened still sounded impossibly loud to her.

She climbed in, again in darkness, as the interior lights were switched off, and forced herself to relax. She leaned across the seats and retrieved the gun from the glove compartment, picking up Steve's machine gun and putting it on the seat next to her. She had little idea how the handgun worked and had forgotten most of the lessons she had been given. She had even less of a clue about the big rifle with its bulbous barrel and telescopic sight. Maybe she would just use it to scare people if she had to.

She started the big diesel engine and cringed at the sudden noise. She didn't wait to see if the engine had attracted attention but drove straight for the trees where she remembered coming in and hoping to find the way south.

Luckily, the Defender was a big, robust vehicle. Her driving had not been great as they headed north, but now it was worse due to the darkness and the fear. She glanced off a few trees and took heavy hits from branches as she swerved through the darkness. After a few hundred metres when the trees closed in, she had to resort to turning on the headlights, which meant stopping to find the switch. The rear lights also had their bulbs removed, so she crept forward with sidelights on at the front and hopefully only the noise of the engine to track her by.

There was no sign of any pursuit, and as she pulled out onto the road, her confidence grew. She put the lights onto full beam and accelerated onto the pitted tarmac as she headed south. She planned to go for as long as she could before hiding the big car off the road. Nervously, she kept glancing in the rearview mirror, expecting the imagined chasers to bear down on her at any minute. She had no idea how long she drove for, frantically checking forwards and backwards for danger. The sun began to rise and the realisation that she had been travelling for hours gave her renewed hope. It also brought a crippling tiredness, making her look for a place to hide.

Steve's distraction worked perfectly. The sentry who was lurking in the shadows watching Emma's tent hadn't seen him creep to the back and whisper to her, but he had heard the noise of his friend arguing with the pilot. His friend was clearly losing, and he had to make a decision: he chose to give his mate backup. Unwittingly, Emma had slipped from the tent no more than five seconds after the soldier had turned away to deal with the valuable pilot. Richards stopped shouting as soon as he made eye contact with Steve. He knew his soldiers were being played.

"Where is the girl?" he barked.

Mitch ran in at that point, and Steve's heart fell at the thought that he had betrayed them and stopped Emma's escape.

"Sir," he said as he stopped short and threw a hasty salute. "Car's gone. Don't know when."

Richards turned to the sentries and fixed them both with a malevolent stare.

"Damn you, both. Get out!" he snarled.

"Sir," they chorused, and fled.

The captain forced himself to breathe and speak calmly.

"Congratulations," Richards said with forced formality as he looked hard into the older man's eyes.

Steve let out a sigh of relief. "I'll fly your helicopter and I'll not try to escape," he said, resigned to his fate. An idea struck him, which he hoped would appeal to this petulant control freak. He slowly took his sidearm from the holster and turned it to present to Richards. "You have my parole," he said formally.

Richards stared at him. Ancient ritual dictated that he should respect the word of a fellow officer and treat him as a gentleman, that he should politely refuse the offer of the surrendered weapon. He was too angry. He snatched the gun from Steve and fought with every muscle in his body not to give in and whip the polished metal hard across his face. He turned on his heel and stalked away in rage.

CHANGE OF PLAN

Pat had to think on his feet. At first he couldn't believe his luck that the first one to come their way was the one who had killed his boy.

That elation soon evaporated when he didn't wake up after the baseball bat had cracked his head. He lay flat on his back, snoring in short shallow breaths. Pat had no idea that the impact of the heavy wood had caused two fractures in Joe's skull and a dislocation of the third and fourth cervical vertebrae. The subdural haematoma was getting larger and putting more pressure on his brain, which had already suffered unrecoverable trauma from the injury and the total lack of care. The spinal dislocation was worsened when they dragged his unconscious body off the road – irreparably paralysing him – and tried to remove the evidence of their ambush.

Pat had watched through binoculars from a round loft window as Dan knelt in the spot where Joe had fallen. He had hoped to extract information from Joe, but his limited medical knowledge put the unconscious man into the category of "completely fucked". He had to evolve his plan to keep ahead of the dangerous man in the middle of his binoculars.

He decided to use the radio and scare them, to threaten them, to let them know they were all dead and that he would be the deliverer of that fate.

He inspected his new weapon, an automatic rifle that he brandished in front of his boys as the weapon that killed one of their own.

He promised it would return that favour, which prompted their cheers, quickly subdued to keep from the noise leading to their detection. He promised a promotion to whoever killed that evil dog too.

He called for hush and climbed into the Land Rover that was hidden inside the barn which had become their temporary headquarters and housed his advance invasion force.

"Are you listening, boyo?" he said into the microphone speaker attached by the coiled wire to the radio on the dash. Silence.

He pressed the button again and chuckled with an evil confidence he summoned from deep within him.

"I know you're listening," he said smoothly, "and I know you're missing a soldier. I warned you this would happen," he finished. He hadn't, but he didn't know who else would be listening either; better to sew a little misinformation into the enemy and have them turn on each other. Still no response.

"I'll be in touch. Sleep well," he said as he replaced the mic.

CONTROLLED RESPONSE

Three people tried to get to the radio at once, forcing Dan to stand in front of it and hold them back. He turned to dial up the volume and tried to listen to the serpentine voice creeping from the speakers.

"QUIET!" he yelled, turning back to look at the radio. He heard the sign off, the threat heavy in the final words.

He turned to the concerned congregation in front of him and had to act fast or suffer a loss of leadership. He had to take charge before too many suggestions were made. Better to do something than nothing.

"Nobody leaves the house. Everyone with training is to be armed at all times," he said, to give himself more time to think. Stating the obvious in a confident manner usually settled the nerves of people who, deep down, just needed to be led. "That was a goad; nothing more. They want us to panic and fracture, as that way we'll be easier to pick off. Everyone spread the word and keep the people calm, but don't give too much detail. Rangers with me, please."

He turned and poured himself a coffee, allowing time for his instructions to be followed without having to stare anyone down. He heard shuffling movement, and after the first gulp of the warm drink, he turned to see Leah, Lexi, Rich, Neil and Marie still standing there.

He opened his mouth to ask them to sit, not contesting Neil's and Marie's presence at all, but was cut off.

"Don't even try to send me out," Marie said. "I need to know what you're planning. I know that look!"

Dan opened his mouth to say he had no intention of banishing her when Neil spoke up.

"And you're down two soldiers with Steve away, so I'm staying too," said Neil.

"Sit down," he said. They sat.

"Marie, I want your input because you're not going to like what I'm going to say. It's safer for me to tell you here so they can protect me." The joke served to soften the atmosphere slightly, but not much. The Rangers stayed silent, not wanting to get in between the two biggest hitters in the room.

"Neil," he said, turning to the man he'd known longest who still lived. "Thank you. We need you. Rich should be able to get you some kit afterwards." He looked at Rich, who gave a single nod. Not a problem.

He resisted the urge to rub his face and scrub away the tiredness and the stress; he must remain in control for all of them to see.

"Leah, Lex, Neil, I need you to rest in shifts and keep sentry on the house. Leah, you have Ash." By deploying his dog to her side, he made it clear that he was going somewhere that required stealth. That wasn't lost on Marie, who sat forward to object to whatever he was planning. He shot her a look, and despite all her fire, she knew when to not push back too far.

"Rich. Your observation point idea is good. Are you up to it?" he said, trying not to look pleadingly at the Marine.

"Not a problem," Rich said with his characteristic can-do style.

"We'll go out on foot and look for activity with night optics. We need to stay out until full light, but it won't be in both directions." That got their attention, as Dan had clearly realised something that the others hadn't. "It's absolutely the right thing to do if we're dealing with trained opposition, but these are amateur thugs; I think they're set up close to where the ambush was."

It was a big gamble, but one that he hoped would pay off. In his own mind, he was sure that Joe was as good as dead already; Patrick's vehement claims about his actions made it clear to him that he had to be seen to punish Joe for killing one of his own, otherwise his pack of feral rats would turn on him. People like that had to show results because their leadership was based on fear and retribution more than respect and confidence in ability.

Dan's purpose now was to find the infestation and clear the nest. If Joe was still alive, then that was good, but he still prepared himself for the worst.

He pulled the map of their area down to the table and showed them where the site was, describing it in as much detail as he could.

"Buildings?" he asked Leah.

The young girl put down her coffee cup and shut her eyes, hands rising from the table as she mimed out the layout from the mental picture she conjured in her mind.

"Walled yard to the left, entrance just before the wrecked cars. Trees and thick hedge to the right, blind crest of the road a hundred metres ahead. Fields each side." She dropped her hands down and opened her eyes, back in the present.

The realisation that such a young person could effectively provide cognitive recall was astounding, even more so that she had never been taught to. Dan supposed it was just another side effect of her upbringing; it didn't cross her mind not to be able to flick through the mental snapshots she had taken.

"So, we need a vantage point without going near the buildings," he said.

"One behind the hedge on the crest and another on the bend in the ditch," said Rich. Dan deferred to him on this, as his experience of setting up OPs and ambushes far outweighed them all collectively.

"OK. Leah, can you break out a set of the old one-to-one radios and earpieces?" he asked. Better to have some form of communication between himself and Rich than risk being discovered when the time came to signal their departure. "There will be no contact between us and the house until we get back in person," he said, hoping that they would get back but not wanting to voice unhelpful fears.

Rich stood to fetch the right equipment with Leah following suit. Neil went with them to arm himself and help load all the spare shotguns for the others. Lexi busied herself with her personal kit, and when that was done, she took away the cold coffee pot and mugs to refresh them, leaving Dan sitting opposite Marie.

Neither spoke first, worrying that the other would say the opposite.

"Be careful," Marie said quietly, breaking the impasse.

"I will. I won't go off fighting a war on my own, I promise," he replied.

"Good," she said, standing, "because I love you, and I don't particularly like the idea of you getting shot." She said this over her shoulder as she left the room to collect a Glock that she had spent painful hours learning to use at his insistence.

NIGHT OPERATIONS

Throughout history, military operations conducted in darkness had produced a number of catastrophic failures and even more needless loss of lives. That was why people like Rich had spent days on end living as an undetected nocturnal killer, both in training and in reality.

Dan was experienced, but not – by any stretch of the imagination – to the degree of a Royal Marine, which was why he wanted Rich with him. He could move silently in the dark, inch by inch, and once told a story of how in training he had crept up to the "enemy" sentry and tied his boots together.

Both wrapped up in camouflage gear and carrying their weapons with a camouflaged net strapped to their small packs, they set off at a jog through the woods in case any small eyes were watching the roads. They had to assume they were. It took them over an hour to reach the fields behind the walled yard with the barn and small shop units. They had no choice but to cross a section of open field, so they waited for the darkness to descend further, discussing tactics and emergency procedures.

"If anything happens, get back to here and wait," Rich said, un-necessarily simplifying the language for an emergency rendezvous point.

"ERV here, roger," Dan replied, gently reminding the Marine that he wasn't a complete novice.

"I'll go for the ditch in the low ground," Rich said in a low voice. Totally professional – he knew that a whisper carried further than a murmur in the dark.

"I'll take the thicket at the crest," Dan replied similarly. "Radios on and earpieces in."

They separated with a bump of their fists – a gesture perpetuated by Leah and curiously infectious – before moving off like predators to their respective targets.

It took them almost an hour to move the less than quarter mile distance. Each movement was measured and controlled, each footfall tentative to test the noise it would make. They settled in and Dan gave a double-click on the radio's press button. He received the rewarding double-squelch in his ear as Rich returned the signal.

In position.

It had been the very first night of their stay at what was now their home when he had last lain prone and still throughout the night, watching and waiting for a threat which was no longer a danger. He settled in, following the almost forgotten routine of wiggling his toes and tensing his muscles all the way up his body to his eyebrows to keep the blood flowing. It kept his mind focused too, kept him alert.

They were rewarded soon afterwards when sounds came from the yard. Slowly, Dan moved the barrel of his carbine towards the houses as the oversized optic drank in all the ambient light it could find to give him an enhanced view. The night-vision goggles were useless at this range; everything after about forty feet was like looking into thick, green fog.

Movement flashed. A person walked between buildings, and the sound of another door reached his ears.

He risked a call to Rich, burying his head down to the ground in the dry leaf mould to muffle any sounds which may escape. "Movement in the barn," he said.

A burst of static preceded Rich's reply. "Male. Pissed against the wall and went back inside," he said.

That had to be them. Anyone staying in a place for any length of time surely wouldn't shit on their own doorstep, literally. No, whoever was in there wasn't planning on staying too long. Feeling a vengeance rise in him, he forced himself to stay calm and not suggest storming the place as he wanted to.

He settled back into his tensing routine, watching and listening. Hours passed by and the glow of dawn began to haze off to his left. Neither of them would get the sun directly in their eyes when it rose. As he was still thinking over plans on how to attack the yard, more movement showed. A scruffy boy was visible in his optic; at this range, he could even see the wispy facial hair he was nurturing.

Dan's breathing froze as the boy turned and looked at him. He knew he couldn't see him, but his eyes were fixed on the thicket he occupied. He began to trudge uphill directly towards him. The radio squelched again in his ear.

"One towards," came Rich's calm and controlled voice.

Dan hit the button twice in positive response. He watched for a painstaking few minutes as the boy got nearer. He didn't want to kill him, not because he was at all squeamish about it but because he knew that a missing boy would provoke the others into action and nullify their advantage. Dan watched him until he got so close that to keep him in his sights would mean too much movement of the barrel. He leaned back slowly, laying the gun flat and rolling onto his left side to draw the suppressed Walther from under him. Keeping his movements very slow, he tried to remain as still as possible. The boy got to within ten feet of him and entered the trees. The foliage was thick before the coming autumn, and Dan was nestled deep inside a patch of weeds in camouflage gear with the net strung over him. He held his breath as the boy looked around to make sure he couldn't see anyone else.

The boy opened his trousers and leaned his left hand against a tree trunk. Dan could hardly believe that he had come all this way to piss against a tree, but he soon realised that this wasn't the purpose to the boy's privacy issues. Even the apocalypse couldn't stop a teenaged boy from having urges, and he was forced to watch in horror as the boy masturbated furiously for almost a minute. He finished and wiped his right hand against the bark of the abused tree before doing his trousers up again and skipping off back down the hill.

Slowly, Dan holstered the sidearm and rolled back onto his front to pick up the carbine again. His earpiece played static before Rich asked the question.

"Dirty little fucker just pulled one off!" Dan said disgustedly.

It didn't come back over the radio, nor did he think Rich would allow a laugh to escape his mouth given their current situation, but he knew he wasn't going to live that one down.

The disgust and comedy of the near discovery was shattered by the next turn of events.

Patrick emerged, M4 brandished on his shoulder like a trophy and pointed at the now useless street lamp by the road. A boy scampered up it like a monkey to drape a piece of rope over the top before sliding back down to land heavily. The rope was arranged, and much to the unbelievable horror of Dan and Rich, it was tied into a loop. There was to be a hanging.

Joe was carried out by six of them, barely able to lift his deadweight. Dan studied him as closely as possible, ignoring the frantic bursts of static from the radio. His skin was a pale grey, his limbs limp and lifeless. A glimpse of his face confirmed Dan's fears; the open eyes told the story.

Joe was dead.

He picked up the radio and spoke softly to Rich.

"He's gone. This is for show." Silence.

"You're sure?" came the only response.

"Positive. I saw his eyes. He's dead."

Another pause, then two bursts of static to acknowledge. They would have to watch their friend be strung up like a piece of meat. If there had been a chance he was still alive, then they would have had no choice but to open up on all of them and risk them getting away.

A speech was given by the fat King as he waved the stolen gun he had no idea how to use. The boys lapped it up as Joe's body was hoisted up and the rope tied to the same car used to trap him. The words of the King were too quiet to reach either of them, and soon after they all went back inside to leave Joe slowly spinning lopsided in the breeze. The anger and the frustration rose in Dan, making him want to march straight down there and kill them all.

The radio came alive.

"Count twenty," Rich said.

Unsure that he could keep his voice calm, Dan gave a double-press to acknowledge.

"Exfil?" Rich asked, wanting to exfiltrate and leave the horrible scene behind them.

He double-clicked again as he carefully secured his equipment and backed out of the hiding place to leave the area via the dead ground out of sight of the yard.

GEOGRAPHICALLY CHALLENGED

Emma was not doing well. She was utterly exhausted and under terrible stress. She craved the safety of the prison but worried that they would blame her for Steve's capture. She hit blockages constantly and spent too long driving in circles. Eventually she got scared when she saw movement when trying to turn the big, unfamiliar vehicle around and fired three shots wildly from the window to scare whoever was there away. The shots served only to deafen her and leave her ears ringing for the rest of the day.

She resorted to using the motorway to make distance south, ever fearful that her pursuers were gaining on her. She didn't even know how much ground she had gained while fleeing south, but each hour, her desperation grew with her panic and the tiredness made her less and less effective.

She wasn't to know, but there was no pursuit. Steve had been kept in an office for two days, being brought breakfast, lunch, and dinner but no word from outside his prison. Nobody had thought to remove his knife or spare magazines, which made him think that he wouldn't be kept like a prisoner for long. His breakfast on the third day was carried in by the smiling Richards, all trace of the volcanic anger from before evaporated.

"Morning!" he said as he placed the tray down. Two meals were on it, meaning that Richards intended to stay and talk to him.

Steve stood and straightened himself. He had no intention of being anything other than cooperative; getting behind the controls of a helicopter was the only way he would make it home. He thought of it as home. It was where his new family was, and they were waiting for him.

"I hope you've forgiven me for the ruse," he said to the captain. "I promised her she could go home," he finished, laying down the gauntlet to see if Richards was still angry.

He was, but he masked it behind his fake smile. "No matter now," he said. "What does matter, however, is you." He jabbed the point of his knife in Steve's direction as he said it.

"Me?" Steve replied cautiously.

"Yes," Richards said through a mouthful of food. "Are you ready to get in the air again?"

Steve smiled and chewed his mouthful before he replied. "Can't wait," he said genuinely.

His Sig was returned to him as a gesture, and plans were made to leave immediately. He was introduced to six engineers who had been pressed into avionics at short notice. A contingent of four soldiers were accompanying them – mostly, he suspected, to watch him. The command of the expedition was officially his; however, the show was really being run by Mitch.

Mitch shouted his orders and the engineering team jumped to obey. The guards and Steve travelled cramped in a military Land Rover while the engineers brought another. The journey took them a full day and night nonstop with regular driver changes. Steve, exempt from the difficult driving due to his prized status, kept quiet and rested the whole journey as well as he could in a cramped car while being jostled.

The hangar was wound open by hand, quicker this time because of the extra manpower. Steve strolled in to inspect the machine, running his hands over the controls. He sat in the pilot's seat and settled himself, feeling the resistance of the pedals. He flicked the pre-ignition switches, finding the helicopter without power. He sighed and climbed out of the figure-hugging seat.

He missed this, he realised. He missed it a lot.

He set the engineering team to the manuals to study them in detail as he and the others set about searching the base. Steve opened the lockers to find himself some new flight gear, finding a set to fit on the third attempt. The small arms locker had already been emptied – not that it mattered, as he was still carrying his Sig.

He found the obligatory setup where water was being boiled for a hot drink and helped himself to a coffee. He sat and bided his time until he was needed to oversee the maintenance of the aircraft.

PEST CONTROL

The former policeman and his former Royal Marine crept slowly out of the area until the trees masked them. As they stretched out their cramped muscles, Dan lit a cigarette, relishing the harsh smoke after denying himself the addiction all night. They picked up into a jog to get back to the house despite their exhaustion.

Leah, Lexi and Neil all waited for them. More coffee was poured for them as they stripped off their gear and relaxed. Marie breezed in and sat, waiting to hear their news, looking uncomfortable with a gun on her hip.

Dan had to get it out of the way. "Shut the door, please," he said softly, hoping his tone would betray the news he had to give. "Joe's gone," he said.

Marie and Lexi both began to cry, Marie hiding her emotions far less than Lexi could. Neil's mouth was held taut as he breathed heavily through his nose in response. The muscles in Leah's cheeks twitched as her teeth were locked tightly together. Dan saw more anger than grief in her stony face as a single tear escaped to roll down her cheek.

"It gets worse. We saw them stringing his body up. It's a goad for us, designed to make us vulnerable. There's maybe twenty of them, possibly a little more, and they're camped in the barn by the ambush site."

Leah sat and spun her laptop around, working the mousepad to bring up the area. "Move in on foot, cutoffs at each end. Main assault goes in at dusk. We can finally use those pyrotechnics too." An evil smile pricked the corner of her mouth.

Simple and impressive plan, Dan thought. "OK. Tonight, then. Thoughts?" he offered, asking people to pick their preferred roles.

"Thunderbird Two," said Neil quietly, meaning that he wanted to use the vehicle-mounted heavy machine gun again.

"Good. Cutoff closest to here, please," Dan said, receiving a nod from Neil in answer.

He turned to Lexi. "Battle rifle and the high ground as the furthest cutoff?" he said to her, meaning that she should take the position he had occupied through the night. He reminded himself to tell her to avoid the big tree there.

"That leaves us three to go in," he said, looking at Rich and Leah.

Marie shifted in her seat, wanting to object on a purely age-related basis against Leah's involvement in the execution of twenty people. She held her tongue.

"Opposition?" Leah asked, and Rich picked up the briefing.

"Approximately twenty. Some small arms, mostly shotguns. There's also Joe's M4 to consider, so they've got at least one full auto," he said.

"Flashbangs are a good idea," Dan said to Leah.

They had kept these in their armoury for a long time, waiting for an appropriate situation to use them. They were a cylindrical grenade which exploded with a concussive noise and a blinding flash before

214

smaller charges flew out and exploded in turn. In confined spaces, they would burst eardrums and sear the retinas of unsuspecting victims, rendering them blind and deaf and therefore much easier to kill.

"We move up at sundown, get in position and hit them," Dan said with finality. Not a hugely detailed plan, but they had far superior weaponry and the element of surprise. "Right. We need a few hours' sleep," he said, nodding to Rich.

Sleep came fairly easily to Dan for a change, betraying the depth of his exhaustion. He woke and checked his watch, showing it to be mid-afternoon. He climbed out of bed and put on the clothing he wore overnight; there was no sense in getting clean clothes covered in blood and suffering the wrath of the laundry team again.

He had a ravenous hunger which needed to be satisfied. Nervous looks and timid questions were given to him as he ate, which he diverted carefully. When he was full, he wandered into Ops with a large coffee. The whole team was there, waiting.

He sat heavily, emotionally drained from seeing his friend – who was his responsibility – dead and desecrated in front of him, and physically tired from the night spent awake. The few hours of restless sleep hadn't helped his mood much.

"Anyone got any more thoughts?" he asked the room in general.

"A hall burning," Leah said blandly.

"A what?" said Neil, giving her a horrified look.

"I read it in a book. It's what the Vikings did. Wait until they are all inside the barn and set it on fire, then kill anyone who runs out," she explained without a hint of emotion.

Simple. Effective. Ruthless.

"OK," Dan said, not in the mood to justify engaging the human rights of the invaders. "Lexi picks off anyone uphill; mark your shots and mind you don't kill us by accident. Us three go in on foot followed by Neil in Thunderbird Two. We light it up and Neil comes reversing in with the big gun."

Nobody raised an objection, just as they hadn't when they agreed to the plan to attack Bronson and his gang of slavers.

"I've got five radios linked," said Rich, surprising Dan by being so alert and finding the time. "Lex, Nikki, Dan, Neil," he said in turn as he passed out each one and kept one for himself.

Marie sat silent, almost as a moral weathervane there to monitor their humanity and ensure they didn't stray too far from acceptability. She found that she had nothing to say; the murder of Joe and her hatred of Patrick had massaged her senses of vengeance and self-preservation.

Over the next hour and a half, they ran through every different scenario they could, something that Dan always encouraged. This way, if something unexpected happened, they had already agreed a way of dealing with it.

As the sun started to sink behind the trees, Dan called a break. They melted away deep in their own thoughts, some to eat and others to rest.

Dan went outside with his dog and his lover for a peaceful smoke in mutually comfortable silence.

MEANWHILE, UP NORTH

Steve sat mostly idle for an entire day as the engineers researched everything they could about the aircraft. They began working on bringing it to life that evening by charging the batteries and flushing the fuel and hydraulic lines.

The following morning, Steve donned his new flight suit and helmet to help.

Eventually, the huge machine whirred and spluttered into life, allowing him to run through the complex pre-flight procedures. They started it, shut it down, and started it again until all the dials showed ready. He tried to think of more reasons to delay and wasted hours on insisting that reserve fuel tanks were removed from other aircraft and fitted to the Merlin.

~

Emma battled her way south, making better distance on some days. Her exhaustion made the days merge into one. She had no idea how long she had been going by herself after the third day; she barely stopped long enough to sleep sufficiently to set her mind straight. She obsessed over Steve's fate and how he had sacrificed his liberty for the chance of her freedom.

On the same day that Steve set about increasing the flight range of the helicopter, she began to try the CB radio as she drove on.

INFESTATION

Dan and Lexi set off on foot as the sun dropped low, with Rich bringing the others over later in Neil's murderous gunship. They knew the timings from their journey yesterday, and Lexi's fitness kept her easily at pace with Dan.

He reached the dead ground and lay in wait with her for the darkness that would allow her to reach her position undetected. Noises of movement and talking reached them intermittently from the target. As the night loomed, Dan withdrew to loop around and wait for the rest of their assault force.

As the last of the light failed, the oversized Defender rolled towards him without lights. Neil stopped and Leah got out with Rich. Ash was sitting in the cab with Neil as planned, ready to hunt down anyone quick enough and unlucky enough to escape the storm of lead soon to be heading at them with supersonic deadliness.

The three crept low and slow towards the target, more noises drifting to their ears from their unsuspecting victims. A young sentry stood bored outside the large doors to the barn, uninterested in the outside world and clearly wishing he was inside with the others. By now, Lexi would be watching Dan's blind aspect of the building through her ambient light scope, using the rising moonlight to enhance her view. At that distance, she was guaranteed to be lethal.

Dan held back the others as he stayed motionless, watching the building.

Amateurs, he thought. Only one sentry. They must believe completely that they were safe despite the occasional light and the low noise coming from the building. It was almost unfair that they were there to exterminate them, but then the sight of Joe's body twirling in the wind obliterated those thoughts and all mercy he could have felt evaporated.

How to discourage a threat? Kill every last one of them. Hurt them so much that they could never hurt you again.

He shuffled slowly backwards and muttered to the others to move up and wait as he crept forward, skirting a wide circle on the ground to avoid his movement attracting any attention. He reached the rear of the barn and watched through a gap as the scruffy collection of teenagers and young men lounged in a false sense of security. A dozen small motorbikes were canted over next to Joe's Land Rover and another car, the faint smell of petrol invading his nostrils from the machines. He listened to their muttered conversation, hearing snippets of their hopes. They anticipated warm beds, hot water, and – most worryingly – their pick of the women. Dan's moral compass pointed true north now, and the justification of the planned mass murder calcified inside him.

He slowly reached into his leg pockets and removed the plastic bladders of petrol, retrieving more from inside his vest and the small bag he carried. Creeping further forward, he began to pour them into the gaps in the wooden slats of the barn walls, hoping the smell of the petrol would be masked by the prevailing odour of the machinery inside until he was finished.

He crept along the side of the barn, turning left and left again to bring him out directly around to the bored sentry. The boy was five feet away, holding a crudely shortened twelve-bore shotgun with the stock and barrels sawn away, totally unaware. Dan melted back behind the wall and covered his face as he brought the small radio up to his mouth.

"Flashbangs on my mark when I take out the sentry. Five… Four… Three," he said, leaving the final two seconds unspoken as he readied his weapon.

He stepped quickly out of the shadows and put a single round through the back of the boy's head, felling him instantly. The boy would never know anything of the assault, but then he should have been watching more attentively.

Before his uncontrolled legs had collapsed his body to the floor, Leah and Rich burst low from the shadows. They each threw a pyrotechnic grenade deep into the barn, cripplingly illuminating the building in noise and light. All three of them kept their eyes closed, and Dan let his weapon hang to press his hands over his ears tightly. They withdrew into the shadows as the last of the explosions left the area in a sudden, stunned silence.

The noise of the Land Rover reversing became louder, just as the first screams emerged from the barn. Flames licked hungrily, casting an eerie light into the yard as the petrol ignited by the grenades searched hungrily for fuel to burn.

Dan ran to join Rich and Leah behind cover on the other side of the yard and heard the first spits of suppressed rounds searching for targets behind him. Some of the group had staggered, blind and deaf, to the door only to be cut down by efficient shots from his burned Marine and child assassin.

Neil roared backwards into the yard, jumping from the vehicle and climbing into the rear bed to load a huge round into the evil machine gun.

A few seconds of bizarre silence engulfed them. Not true silence – cries of panic and pain emanated from the barn over the crackling of the spreading flames.

Neil decided to kick the hornet's nest, stitching two bursts into the timber walls by way of encouragement. Dan, Leah and Rich responded to his help by felling each of those frightened by the heavy fire. They dropped, hit by three different marksmen every time. Shouting could be heard from inside now, a man's voice bellowing orders. The sound of breaking timbers echoed out, indicating at least some shred of collective intelligence as the choking occupants tried to force their way out through the rear wall.

Lexi saw them. The first timber to fall away showed a bright slash of firelight, and she put two bullets directly into the fresh breach in their walls. That ended their attempts to escape that way, forcing the trapped rats to turn and attack.

Shotguns were fired from the doorway, foolishly enticing the heavy machine gun to respond and shred them through the thin walls. More instructions were bellowed, and a final attempt at escape was organised. As one, the survivors burst from the door and scattered. The hope that sheer numbers would protect them was a naïve one as the efficient fire picked them all off.

"ENOUGH!" cried a deep adult voice from inside.

Dan snatched at his radio and called for them to cease fire. He called them all by name to ensure that they had their fingers off their triggers. "COME OUT," he yelled, smiling with satisfaction as a soot-stained and sweating King of Wales stepped forward. He had Joe's M4 in his left hand, held by the barrel to indicate that he was no threat.

Dan stood and walked towards him, meeting face to face in the middle of the flame-lit yard. Patrick was beaten and scared. More scared than he had probably ever been. Dan walked around him slowly, taking the M4 from his unresisting hand. He reached inside Patrick's belt and withdrew the Glock; both stolen weapons being retrieved felt symbolic to Dan. His ideas for symbolism grew. He walked to the barn and braved the growing heat to force the large doors closed, trapping anyone left inside.

Afterwards, that kept him awake with the cruelty of such a death.

Realising what he was doing, Patrick roared "NO" and tried to rush him.

Dan responded by delivering a huge kick to his chest, knocking him flat on his back. Patrick rose with difficulty, fighting for breath but full of anger. He raised his fists and tried to control his face from opening the gates to the tears he held back, foolishly thinking that there were rules to their conflict anymore.

Dan delivered another savage kick to the side of his right knee, pivoting on his left leg to add the full weight of his power, dropping him back to the ground. As Patrick knelt before him, Dan considered using the butt of his carbine to end him, but he left him there, watching the remnants of his leadership burn more intensely.

Leah and Rich came forward to flank the fat, broken man as Dan walked slowly towards where Joe remained suspended. He untied the knots and lowered him to the floor as gently as he could, forcing the thin rope out of the cold, swollen flesh of his neck. Neil helped him put the body of their friend into the back of the Defender, carefully lowering him onto the hot brass of the expended bullets.

Dan turned to Leah and Rich. "Bring him here," he said coldly.

Sensing his fate, Patrick began to speak for the first time. He tried to throw himself onto his back, shouting "NO" repeatedly.

Leah twisted the hand and wrist of his left hand behind him, bracing his arm painfully straight, forcing him up to his knees and then his feet as he tried to resist the pain in his wrist, elbow and shoulder. Using both hands, she forced the straight arm forward, making Patrick walk as he bent over in agony.

Feebly, he tried to plead with them and finally allowed the tears to stream down his face without shame.

Rich spat in his face as he went by; Neil watched on with an unreadable expression.

"Your Highness," Dan said with utter seriousness and dripping with mock deference, "for your crimes, you have been sentenced to death."

Before any response could come, he snatched up the looped end of the rope and threw it over Patrick's head. He fought, causing a painful-sounding *crack* from his wrist as Leah increased the pressure and forced him back to his knees. She held him there and nodded to Dan. He picked up the other end of the rope, and helped by Rich and Neil, they slowly hauled the fat monarch to his feet.

Leah let go of her now useless restraint and stepped smartly back out of reach of the legs which now began to thrash wildly as his feet cleared the ground. Slowly he rose, foot by foot, as the three heavy men hauled on the rope.

The screams became choked sounds of pain and panic, quickly becoming gasps and sounds of dying. He dangled there, suffocating as his ridiculous girth combined forces with gravity to end his evil life.

His last thoughts were of the meagre upbringing in a small village, of his mother and absent alcoholic father whose only parenting was to deliver beatings when the mood took him, and of the life of drifting and petty crime. He had many memories and more regrets from his dull existence; the best times he had enjoyed were after the more successful people in the world had all gone.

He had so many wishes in his life and childish dreams of happiness, but the last thought he ever had was a memory of Dan telling him that if he came back, he would kill him.

The kicking stopped and the eyes grew wide just as the liquid ran down his legs and dripped from his boots. The hands haltingly fell away from the cord which killed him.

WHERE IS MY FRIEND?

They stood in silence and watched the barn burn as Patrick turned slowly left and right on the end of his rope. Nobody said a word. Leah, efficient as ever, reloaded her carbine to ensure a full magazine was in place.

Two loud shots rang out from up the hill, sparking them all into sudden defensive action until their radios all crackled simultaneously.

"Last one," said Lexi. "Coming down."

She joined them at a jog about a minute later, taking in the close-up of the former King without comment. She had witnessed their friend being lowered and the fat murderer replacing him and she wasn't bothered. As far as she was concerned, he deserved it, and that was the end of the matter.

"What were the last two shots?" Dan asked her, curious.

She looked to the floor, unsure how to explain without sounding judgemental. "One came out the breach at the back. He was burning, so I…" She trailed off. Dan nodded to her. He was glad she put whoever it was out of their misery. Nobody deserved to burn to death, he thought hypocritically as the burns on his hands started to hurt. He hadn't noticed until now, but multiple blisters were forming where he had manhandled the burning wood to shut the doors and end the lives of everyone left inside.

They stood in silence, watching the flames engulf the barn and begin to melt the closest cars and structures. He realised that Joe's Defender was incinerated too, not that it mattered, as they had another seven wrapped up under tarpaulins in a closed barn on the farm. Still, it was Joe's, and now it was dead too.

Dan had the familiar waves of guilt wash over him: had he trained Joe well enough? Was Joe prepared for any of this? He shook it off. Joe was good enough; he had proven that when the fat bastard Patrick had driven up on him months ago. One man, his man, had shamed them and got away with four women safely. The fault was his own. He shamed Patrick when he came to ask for guns as the cost for his dead boy. He threatened him and sent him away.

It was Dan's fault that they had come for retribution, and Joe had paid the price.

Dan produced his cigarettes and lighter from the custom pocket on his vest, but involuntarily cried aloud when his rapidly swelling hands couldn't work the lighter. He dropped the lighter, breathing heavily with the cigarette still in his mouth. Silently, Leah picked it up and lit the cigarette, putting the lighter back in the pouch.

"Let's get you to Kate," she said gently to him. "Let's get back," she called out to the others, louder and full of confidence. They all turned to the Land Rover unquestioningly, accepting her leadership implicitly.

Dan climbed in the back, his eyes resting on the body of Joe for the journey. Leah rode with him, perched opposite with watchful eyes never leaving him. Without warning, the vehicle slowed and stopped, rocking the rear passengers uncomfortably and making Dan reach out to steady himself, causing his teeth to grind with the pain in his hands.

"Say again?" he heard Neil say into the CB radio. "Hello?"

"What's going on?" Dan asked through the small window in the bulkhead.

"Something on the radio," Neil said, "couldn't make it out but it was female and panicked."

He looked at Leah, eyes wide. "Emma?" he asked her.

Leah banged on the roof of the cab. "Get back to the house, now!" she said with force.

Neil drove hard, pulling up within a couple of minutes. Leah bundled out over the side and yelled for Kate. The medical team must have been waiting, fearing the worst, as Alice burst from the door with a trauma kit in her hands.

Leah headed her off. "Dan has minor burns, nothing serious," she said as she strode inside.

She emerged seconds later, twirling car keys in her hands. "Neil, Lexi, lock this place down. Rich, with me."

Dan stood dumbstruck as they all jumped to obey her instructions. She looked at him, grabbing his shoulder to emphasise her point. "You stay here. I'm borrowing your dog." She gave one sharp whistle, prompting Ash to jump down from the gunship and cast a look to his owner.

Dan told him to get on, twitching his head towards Leah. He was still in shock as the girl jumped behind the wheel of his own Discovery after letting his dog in the back seat and watching Rich climb into the passenger's side. He looked on with incredulous awe as she gunned the three-litre engine and shot away into the dark in his car with a chirp of the big tyres and his dog grinning out of the side window.

"No, no," he muttered with false deference, "take my car. I insist!"

In a rare moment of obedience, Dan allowed himself to be led inside, stripped of his gear, and receive treatment for the rapidly worsening burns on his hands.

"What have you been doing to yourself?" Alice asked as she held Dan's hands in a bowl of cold water.

~

Leah drove hard, heading for the motorway where she first made her solo appearance in the world since she was the frightened little girl who spent the night in a Land Rover dealership all that time ago. Rich, on instruction, was using the CB every few seconds as Leah wove the big car further and further north.

"The house wasn't picking anything up, so we must be at the extreme of the signal range. Keep trying."

He did.

Leah had also had the forethought to grab a large-scale Ordnance Survey map, just in case. They had been moving for less than six minutes before Leah turned a hard hairpin back onto the motorway where she had rammed the car and killed a man who threatened those she loved.

She loved Dan dearly. She had never really had a father, not since the one who had actually fathered her had preferred drugs and fighting to being her dad. Dan was her dad, but she was too embarrassed to ask to call him that. That's why she was doing this now, so that he didn't have to go out injured. If he couldn't even light one of his silly smelly cigarettes, then how could he perform a tactical reload under fire? No, she had to do this and do it fast.

She pushed the big 4x4 into a sweeping bend on the motorway, reaching over ninety-five miles an hour and squeezing the accelerator to keep the big automatic settled and sat down squat into the turn. As the road levelled out, a burst of static disrupted the radio.

"…know where I am…please…me…anyone there?"

Emma, and not a happy Emma.

Rich was quick to respond. "Emma? Is that you? Can you hear me?" he fired back.

"…Hello?"

"Find out where she is," Leah said, concentrating on the pitch-black road illuminated by the bright headlights.

Rich spent the next five minutes trying to exchange conversation between them, until Leah crested a hill on the motorway and the signal suddenly became clear.

She stopped fast, flicking the dial between the front seats to select R and launching backwards to the top of the hill.

The signal came through loud and clear.

"Emma? Emma?" she said after snatching the mic from Rich.

"Hello?" Emma answered.

"It's Leah. Tell me *exactly* where you are," she barked with more authority than any thirteen-year-old had the right to own.

She did, to some extent.

Leah flicked on the internal LED light and bathed the cab with unnaturally harsh bright light. She threw open the map and exchanged a few more lines with Emma, until she was sure where Emma was. As luck would have it, they were on the same motorway but about twenty miles apart.

"Roll slowly. We're coming to get you. Flash your lights when you see us," Leah said, flicking off the interior light and dropping the big car into drive before planting the accelerator into the carpet.

Best-laid plans and all; they hit a complete roadblock after two miles. She had no idea, but it was the same roadblock Emma's attackers had planned to trap her against when she bumbled into their lives. Leah had to get out and check the blockage before deciding that one car could easily be dragged out to make a gap wide enough for the Land Rovers.

She quickly hooked up the front winch and dragged a wreck of an old Subaru clear as Rich scanned the area with his rifle. The cable was rapidly withdrawn and the journey resumed. They found Emma after another fifteen minutes.

She saw them approaching fast and flashed her headlights, causing a sudden flash in the eyes of her rescuers.

Leah pressed the handbrake button after flicking the selector into park and burst from the driver's door. As she feared, Emma was alone. She was a complete state, with a grimy face and messy hair.

"Steve? Where's Steve?" she barked, scanning around with the dog at her left heel and her carbine raised out of paranoid habit.

Emma could barely speak.

Leah took charge, asking Rich to drive the Defender back as she led Emma to the passenger's seat of the Discovery. As confident as she seemed to the others, all she wanted to do was get this mess back to Dan to decide what to do.

The two-car convoy moved fast, eager to be off the road and back in the relative safety of home.

Emma didn't say a word; she just hugged her knees and rocked slightly.

"Where's Steve?" Leah asked again, forcing herself to sound calmer.

"It's not my fault," Emma said weakly.

Fearing the worst, Leah just drove on with the need to get home.

Dan's burns were worse than he realised and had started to blister badly. Kate had run them repeatedly under cold water and wrapped his swollen hands in wet bandages. He was starting to feel the pain when Lexi poured three very healthy measures of single malt for them as she, Dan and Neil sat at the table in Ops. Dan reached for the CB mic but dropped it due to the ungainliness of his alien hands.

Neil stood and picked it up. "You there, young'un?" he broadcast.

"Yeah. On the way back. One on board," she said.

Dan heard the stress in her voice even if the others didn't.

"One?" Neil said.

"Yes, yes. Ten minutes," she replied.

True to her word, nine minutes later she pulled up and nosey-parked his car, closely followed by Rich climbing out of Steve's Defender. No Steve.

Emma did not look good; she was physically exhausted and was half carried by Leah inside. Emma raised her eyes and looked directly at Dan.

"Please," he said through anger made far worse by the pain, "tell me where my goddamned Ranger is."

ALIVE

Before she lost consciousness, Emma managed to tell them he wasn't dead.

That was good, Dan supposed. The events leading up to him being alive and not there still needed explaining in detail, but Kate was adamant that the girl needed at least some rest before they interrogated her.

She was awake by lunchtime, before Dan woke, resulting in Marie carefully rousing him. The exhaustion and stress of the last thirty-six hours coupled with the painful blisters on his hands and the subsequent painkillers had knocked him out cold.

She helped him into some uncharacteristically comfortable clothes and led him downstairs. He allowed her to take control of him – welcomed it, in fact. There had barely been a day during the last year when he hadn't been worrying about himself and everyone else, about their future and the threats to their safety. The few times he hadn't been thinking like that were when he had been ill or injured. Fearing what he would hear, he sat in Ops and accepted a coffee as he watched Emma fidgeting in her seat. She had showered and her now clean hair hung damply as she bent her head to her drink.

"Are you OK?" Dan asked her as he shifted in his seat for comfort, remembering his lack of manners and concern when he saw her last.

"Yes, thank you," she replied timidly. She cleared her throat and set her drink down on the table carefully, preparing herself to recite the story of the last few weeks.

Nobody interrupted her until she reached the part about Richards. Dan sat forward and fired off a series of questions designed to establish the basis of a threat assessment. It was automatic.

"Debrief later," Leah instructed. "Go on," she gently urged the scientist ten years plus her senior, putting Dan in his place.

She told them of the escorted visit to the lab, of the inconclusive blood tests, and then of the discovery of the computer login details.

Dan fought to control his impatience and stop it boiling over into temper; he didn't care one bit about the science right now and wanted to know what had happened to his friend. He couldn't wait any longer. "Later. Steve?" he said, trying not to snap.

"We got back to the army camp. Richards wasn't going to let us go, so Steve got me out and stayed. He said he was the real prize, that they wouldn't chase me if he stayed," she blurted out, worried that she would be blamed for his absence.

"That sounds like Steve," Dan said, "but what was his plan to get out?"

Steve had to have an exit strategy, Dan thought. He was too clever and analytical to just sacrifice himself.

"He's going to fly back," she said simply, silencing them all.

FIVE HUNDRED FEET

The large bladder tanks replaced two of the folding seats on each side of the helicopter, allowing the side doors to still be used. The hydraulics controlling the ramp decided to stop working, resulting in a further day's delay while the problem was diagnosed and fixed. Having the rear ramp up wasn't exactly necessary to fly, but the excuse kept them grounded for long enough to lose the daylight.

Finally, Steve could stall no further. Pre-flight checks were normal, all dials were in the green, and he agreed to try and take her up the next morning into a hover before bringing the aircraft back to earth.

The first test flight made his nerves taut with fear. He expected cockpit alarms to sound at any second and for the engines to stall, plummeting him down to his death.

He didn't die, nor did the old Merlin falter.

Steve's elation almost made him forget that he was there under duress, albeit with faked compliance. He insisted on taking her up again, this time unable to stop volunteers from joining him. A nervous mechanic named Phil wanted to come up, and Mitch joined them. The soldier helped strap Phil in and put a headset on him, giving a thumbs up to save shouting over the noise of the whining engines.

Mitch wore a harness like the straps for a parachute, shoulders and legs held tight, and a heavy strap attached to a clip to secure him as the stand-in loadmaster. He attached it inside the doorway and spoke into the boom mic on his headset. "Let's take her up," he said.

Steve manipulated the controls to launch the helicopter up and backwards, quickly getting clear of the ground. He banked hard, making Mitch brace himself in the open side door.

"How are we looking, Mitch?" Steve asked, wishing he was alone and could flee south.

"All good," came the crackling reply. "Phil's not enjoying it, though!" he said with amusement, looking at the terrified mechanic.

"I'll do a quick sweep and take her back down," Steve said.

"Are we not heading south now?" Mitch asked.

Steve's smile evaporated. "South?" he asked, feigning ignorance.

"I assumed that's where we were headed, to find your people? Why else do you think I'm here with Phil, who's shit-scared of flying?" Mitch said with a laugh.

Steve couldn't believe it. His secret plans of escape were obvious to Mitch, who had even established a fellow deserter to join them.

Richards's happy ship was taking on water, it seemed.

He laughed aloud to himself at his own stupidity; of course people suspected he would run. Why else were so many "guides" sent to "protect" them?

Well, that plan just backfired. He was in the air, he was free, and he was heading home.

The remaining guards and engineers on the ground watched in ignorant admiration as the old bird banked and flew a ponderous loop over their small base. They remained fixed in their gaze at the empty sky as the aircraft levelled out and dipped its nose to raise the tail end and surge over their heads. It took them over a minute to start to really worry. When the noise of the three turboshaft engines had faded into eerie silence, the first serious doubts gnawed at them.

One by one, they realised that the helicopter which had taken them a few days to nurse back into flight-worthiness was gone, and that they had been made complete fools of.

The last of the soldiers to stay watching the sky sighed to himself, not relishing the punishment he would likely receive when he got back to the captain.

He let his gaze drop from the sky and sighed again to himself.

"Oh shit," he said to nobody in particular.

"You're deserters!" Steve joked with Mitch and Phil.

"Technically not," reasoned Mitch as he braved the buffeting side winds to close the sliding door in the fuselage. "I'm defecting if you think about it. So is Phil, aren't you, mate?"

Steve couldn't see behind him, but his headset relayed Phil's pained croak of response. He didn't think Phil gave much of a shit right now; he would probably start throwing up soon.

Mitch stood behind Steve's shoulder in the doorway to the cock-pit and leaned against the wall as he still held the metal rail above his head.

"Like a Russian spy or something," he explained.

Steve smiled, glad for the company and the welcome turn of events.

He flew low and hard, hugging the contours of the ground and going no higher than five hundred feet from the undulating earth below. He avoided the larger hill ranges, skirting to the east or west to save having to gain altitude. His hands and feet were as one with the controls, his very soul hardwired into the machine. Not once did the smile leave his face as he accelerated close to a hundred and eighty miles an hour.

They discussed the smoking ruins of a burned-out population centre in the distance, with Mitch remarking that it was likely improved and far safer than it had been a couple of years ago. Steve picked up the snaking tarmac as it widened to four lanes and followed it south, knowing that within half an hour it would merge with another tarmac artery of their now deceased country. He could follow that new road right to the doorstep of the prison and be landing minutes later. He daydreamed about the looks on their faces and hoped that Emma had got back safely by now.

He brought his thoughts back to the present, thinking in wonder about how they were still in the air as he had switched off completely for a number of seconds; he had done that in a car so many times and didn't crash, but somehow doing it in ten tonnes of screaming jet engines and spinning metal made any lapse in concentration even more dangerous.

He pushed on, ignoring the ache creeping into his legs and arms and shoulders. He was out of practice physically, but that didn't detract from his deeply ingrained ability or skill in piloting the bird over the overgrown wasteland below.

YOU CAN'T PARK THAT THING THERE

Dan began to give a flurry of orders for maps to be found and the site identified. He fired question after question at Emma, ignoring her vulnerability in his own selfishness and upsetting her.

Of course she didn't know what weapons were what; she couldn't tell a submachine gun from a duck gun, so his interrogation caused her stress. She broke, crying and apologising for coming back alone.

Dan finally realised he was being a complete dick. He stood, placing one bandaged hand awkwardly on her shoulder. "I'm sorry," he said. "I'm glad you're back safe, and if I were Steve, I would have done anything to get you out too."

She softened at that.

In truth, he was very worried about Steve, and even more worried about the thought of taking on a group of soldiers to get him back with their depleted force. He went outside to smoke, followed by Marie, who lit the cigarette for him. He was saved the remonstration from Marie about how harshly he had treated Emma when Neil appeared with Chris and Ewan.

"It's time," Neil said, face cast in a stony expression of sorrow. They had dug the hole and planted a large stone ready for Joe's burial.

"OK," said Dan quietly, pausing to draw on the cigarette again. "Get everyone out."

He and Marie left the trio and walked slowly towards the spot in the woods where Penny's well-tended grave stood among the flowers. The hole was deep and neat, the excavated earth piled tidily by the side partially in the shadow of the large piece of natural sandstone standing proudly as a headstone. Joe was already inside, wrapped tightly in a sheet.

They waited in silence as the others slowly and silently gathered around them. Dan worried that he wouldn't be able to give any kind of speech; he felt too empty, too forlorn and too angry. He felt right now that their life was pointless and they would have been better off being one of the lucky ones who weren't immune. He'd certainly experienced more pain since it had happened than he would have if the virus had killed him.

Soon, almost their whole contingent was present. Dan recognised nearly all of them but could probably only name half if pushed.

Neil cleared his throat and looked at him expectantly, prompting the unofficial ceremony to begin.

Dan just couldn't bring himself to force out the words he didn't believe right now. He knew it was a mixture of the grief, the pain, the exhaustion and probably the strong tablets Kate had given him.

Marie sensed this somehow and stepped forward to stand on the raised slope behind the graves. "Joe died to protect us," she sang out in her clear voice, instilling instant silence and feeling the burning attention of so many eyes. "He did his job. He did it well." She paused to look down at the wrapped body below her. "Those who killed him knew with their final breath what it meant to cross us. To kill us. To attack us." Her eyes scanned the crowd, reading them as she did and encouraging the collective heartbeat to quicken to her words. "But this isn't what makes us special, what makes us *more*." She invested the last word with heavy emphasis, showing the crowd a clenched fist to underline her point. "We are a society. We are a family. Today, we mourn the loss of one of our soldiers, our brother. Our friend. But we are here and we are free to mourn because of his sacrifice."

All eyes were fixed on her.

She seized the opportunity. "As you may know, we are missing another soldier. Another brother. Another friend. As we pray for the soul of Joe to find rest, so too do we hope for the safe return of Steve."

She stooped to collect a small handful of earth from the mound and held her arm out straight, slowly trickling the dark soil between her fingers to fall on Joe's body. She gently took Dan's arm and led him away, saving him the need to add any words or try and use his swollen hands to throw dirt on his friend. The others followed suit, mimicking her actions one by one as they formed a solemn queue to pay their respects and disperse to their own thoughts.

Dan kept his gaze on the ground and his expression plain as she led him back to the house, intending to insist he rested. They stood near the house and smoked in silence again.

Ash's ears pricked up. He turned his head to face the woods, swinging it back and forth between the house and the farm, searching. They watched the dog in companionable silence, neither switching on to what the animal's behaviour meant. It was only the low rumbling growl of the patented early warning system that sparked Dan's return to the present.

He instinctively reached for a weapon, realising he wasn't – for the first time in as long as he could remember – carrying one.

He threw down his half-smoked cigarette and bawled for Leah and Rich and Lexi. In his grief, he almost called for Joe too, then remembered and felt another surge of anger.

Why won't people just leave us alone? he thought. His feelings of uselessness made him colour up in frustration that his burned hands couldn't work a weapon, that he would have to leave the defence of their home to others.

People were running past them in panic just as the noise began to break through the trees: the high-pitched whine of the engines and the unmistakable *whop, whop, whop* of rotor blades. Dan could barely believe what he was hearing. They had no time to react, to form a defence.

With a huge, invasive noise, the dull green helicopter burst over the tops of the trees and banked in a lazy circle before it levelled out and lowered itself to the open field to Dan's right.

They all stood in stunned silence, watching as it settled heavily onto its wheels. The engines were cut. Three men emerged from the side door, dropping to the ground and running low towards the house to avoid the wash from the decelerating blades above them.

Steve straightened as he approached them, a broad smile showing on his face from the exhilaration of escape and the excitement of flying again. Dan stood mute, mouth open and speechless. Ash's tail wagged uncontrollably, making his whole back end move until he could contain himself no more and he ran to the familiar pilot, who strode straight up to Dan and embraced him.

So many questions fought for space in Dan's head, none of them making the connection to leave his mouth with any coherence.

"Did Emma make it back?" Steve asked, full of concern.

Dan could only nod in response, still unable to add up everything he had just seen and felt and work out the solution.

The two new men were introduced; Mitch Andrews was a soldier and Phil was a very unwell-looking mechanic. It all washed over Dan; he was suddenly so very tired. Marie made his excuses and led him inside to put him to bed.

Neil stepped forward and shook Steve's hand. He turned to Phil and welcomed him with a handshake and a broad smile. "I hope you know how that thing works," he said in his public-schooled spitfire pilot accent, "because I'm not changing the bloody oil on it!"

FACTORY RESET

Dan slept all afternoon and late into the next morning. His hands were itching badly. Kate examined the wounds and applied a salve to them, telling him to keep the raw skin well moisturised and mobile. They felt better, but he was careful not to break the blisters that were still intact. He wandered downstairs, full of hunger and in desperate need of caffeine.

The mood was definitely higher than yesterday, with the newcomers and Steve being pressed for information about anything and everything. Dan gave the main gaggle a wide berth and headed for Ops where Leah had the duty, kept company by his dog.

"Morning, boss," she said, pouring coffee into his cup.

He sat down, working his sore hands open and closed slowly as Ash nuzzled into him for attention. He stroked the dog's head and looked at Leah.

"Lexi is over at the gardens. Rich went up to the farm and is checking the grounds out. I gave Steve the day off. The new guy wants a spot too," she reported.

Dan assumed the new guy was the soldier and not the mechanic. It would be good to have another trained man on the books, and the fact that they were now one Ranger down went without saying.

Kate had insisted that Dan take a couple of weeks off. There was a time when he would have argued against that, even ignored it completely. He didn't argue, but he would still be involved. He felt relieved with Steve back, elated that he had brought more people to them, and amazed to see him return in a working helicopter. The possibilities were endless for as long as it stayed serviceable.

Steve found him shortly afterwards. He went over the whole story, giving the answers to the questions Dan had previously fired at Emma. Together, they made a full threat assessment of Richards's group and ruled out any interaction; they were simply far too powerful to mix it with, as any loss was unacceptable.

Steve gave his rundown of Mitch, describing him as a confident soldier with a great deal of sense. He laughed as he described how Mitch knew all along what he planned and chose to come with him but didn't risk himself by saying so until it was happening. Steve supported him being on the team.

Dan agreed to speak with him, as he always intended to. He put Steve in interim charge of Ops, insisting that off-site parties went in pairs until further notice. Normal routines were established again and the world turned as it had before.

Mitch came to find him the next morning, engaging in an almost comical replication of Rich's interview.

"Morning, sir," he said as he marched in, stamped to attention and cracked off a crisp salute.

Dan smiled and sat down. "I'm amazed Steve didn't tell you that we don't do sirs and salutes here," he said with amusement.

"He did," Mitch said with a smile. "That's why I did it!" He sat down, pleased with his icebreaker.

"What's your service history?" Dan asked.

"Sixteen years. Infantry Sergeant, despite a demotion once for clocking an eighteen-year-old officer off duty. Parachute trained. I've seen active service in Northern Ireland three times, the Gulf twice, the Balkans, and Afghanistan a couple of times. Not to mention the contacts I've had since all this." He gave his list of achievements casually, making out that eight active tours were nothing. It was something. He went to war six times and he could still smile.

His credentials hardly needed testing, since Steve had seen his work firsthand. Still, Dan was encouraged by the man's humour and didn't want to sign him up without prying further.

"Why desert, then?" he needled.

"Didn't desert. I defected!" he said with a wide smile as he produced a sheaf of papers. "Full Int report on Richards's group. All the gen right here," he declared, using Army slang as if it was his first language. He placed the intelligence package on the table and kept his flat hand on top of it. "So, as soon as I give you this, I'm officially a defector. Vote of no confidence in my leadership, shall we say." Dan returned his smile, but Mitch surprised him by getting serious. "I'm nobody's enforcer; it started out alright when we were rescuing people and defending ourselves, but after that, I began to have doubts. I had to make people stay whether they wanted to or not, and that didn't sit right with me. When I got the gig keeping an eye on Steve, I didn't know what to make of the orders to bring him back at all costs. I got to know him and he told me a lot about you and what you've built here. I want to be a part of something like this instead of being the right hand of a dictator."

He had intentionally raised his standing in Richards's group of loyal supporters, if for nothing else other than to brag about his worth. He needn't have bothered, as Dan had learned everything he needed to know about the man from Steve. He was trained, he was capable, and he had helped both of them escape. He was in.

Mitch looked him in the eye as Dan pretended to think it over. Dan leaned forward to him, returning the stare with similar intensity. "Do you like sweets, Mitch?" he asked, breaking the spell and confusing the soldier.

"Yeah…" he replied cautiously.

Dan leaned back and shouted Rich's name, prompting the Marine to emerge from his den of worship to the god of muzzle velocity.

"Boss?" he asked as he entered.

Dan's smile widened. "Bootneck, Squaddie. Squaddie, Bootneck." He introduced them, demonstrating his own knowledge of inter-military terminology. "Show our new recruit around our sweetie shop, will you?"

Mitch stood, shook Dan's hand – making him tense his face to cover the reactive wince caused by the still painful burns – and went to talk guns with Rich.

Over the next week, Dan finally took the time to move among the group, reacquainting himself with some and hearing about their lives. He visited the medical team daily. His burns weren't bad, but for once he allowed himself to take a back seat and heal slowly.

Ana and Cara were both showing heavily now. With everything that had happened to threaten their group, he had almost forgotten that two new souls were soon to be added to their population count.

He took the time to sit with them and talk when he could, feeling their nervousness and excitement at their imminent arrivals.

Emma and Marie were waiting for him one morning. Emma wanted to tell Dan more detail about what she found at the lab, yet another thing that had slipped his mind.

She opened her laptop and sat opposite them, formal and quiet.

"I found the lab and we got it running again," she said, thankfully skipping all the preamble with the facts that they already knew. "I spent three days checking the blood samples from infected and immune alike; there were no differences." She looked at them both for signs they understood, but explained the obvious anyway. "We all have it. I don't have the expertise or the tools to test further and find out why we are immune, nor do I know how it will affect us in other ways," she paused, "but I do now know what it was."

She opened the files on her laptop, explaining about the science base deep in the Arctic ice. The videos were played for them as they sat in silence, ending with the lab video and the subsequent reports. She closed the laptop slowly and looked at them, folding her hands gently on the table.

"So you're saying that some pollen from a prehistoric flower caused this?" Marie asked.

"Yes. The pollen infected the scientists and must have mutated – I'm theorising from here, you understand. That mutation became an airborne virus with very fast gestation and the highest lethality ever seen in the history of the human race. It's everywhere, and it would have covered the planet in days. There's no going back."

Dan shifted in his seat, working his hands to relieve the tight skin. "Keep theorising," he said gently. "What does this mean for us?"

She sighed heavily, looking down at the table and rubbing her eyes before she looked at them. "I don't know," she answered.

They both looked away in frustration.

"I don't know," she said again with more confidence, "but I'm worried that it may still be our extinction event."

THE HARSH TRUTH

As time moved on, not a single shot was fired at anything other than food throughout the end of summer, autumn and into winter. Christmas approached again, and the excitement of the previous year returned, albeit to a slightly lesser degree. They had reverted to their more relaxed hibernation mode as befitted the shorter days and bad weather.

Both Ana and Cara were nearing their due dates, although exact dates were no longer a sure thing, as the accuracy of maternity services had been greatly reduced since the world had changed forever.

Cara went first. In the middle of the night, half the household got woken up as the wailing woman was helped downstairs to medical. The noise went on, getting louder over the next few hours. This would be Cara's second baby, so she at least knew something of what to expect. Kate's team had spent months preparing for this, researching and practising as much as they could for when the time came.

Dan lay awake with Marie, listening to the muffled urgency of the noises from the floor below them. It was still well before daybreak when Dan was forced from the cosy bed to use the bathroom. He wrapped up warm, slipping his feet into his unlaced boots, and decided to take his dog outside in the hope that he would give them even a slight lie-in if he was given a toilet break too.

He stood there, watching the annoyingly alert animal water the tyres of three different vehicles. The sounds inside were reaching a painful crescendo every few minutes, and Dan expected the sounds of a baby's cries to soon echo among the big rooms and high ceilings.

Unable to bear the sounds of Cara's pain any longer, he went back inside and climbed back into bed, annoying Marie with his cold hands. He must have dozed off again after a while, waking again when Marie was forced from the warm bed to retrace his steps from earlier.

His bliss was ended when she burst back into the room in tears. "The baby," she said in panic, her hand clasped to her mouth, "it died."

She threw herself onto the bed and hugged him tightly, her tears soaking his neck as she sobbed.

It turned out that the labour was fairly normal, but the baby hadn't moved throughout. Eventually, the baby was born, but it wasn't breathing. It was underdeveloped, and Kate suspected that it had died in the womb over a week ago.

Dan sat with her late that night with a drink and heard Kate's worries.

"I hadn't heard a heartbeat for almost ten days, but without the ability to do a C-section, there was nothing I could do," she admitted, having told nobody else and feeling better for sharing the burden she had carried alone until now.

Cara was sedated in medical and Matty looked after the kids. He was upset, understandably, but kept it together to keep his two adopted children as steady as he could. Two days after the stillbirth, the baby – who Cara had named Evie – was buried next to Penny and

Joe. A smaller stone, rough and naturally white in colour, marked the tiny grave. The group was quiet, subdued.

Ana was terrified. She went into labour five days later. She writhed in pain, screaming for hours on end. Kate's exhausted team stayed with her for a day and a half. Chris was distraught, his frustration and fear eventually making Kate insist he left medical and allow them to work. He refused, and the screams of pain were drowned out by his shouting.

Dan had to intervene, and Chris's panic was so accentuated that Dan was forced to hold him in a painful restraint to remove him. Chris apologised sincerely, and eventually the anger and frustration dissolved into tears. Dan drank with him for a while and tried his hardest to keep him diverted. Marie took over after a while, allowing Dan a much-needed break, and she convinced Chris to sleep for a while on the settees in the lounge.

Kate opened the door a crack to look out. Marie saw her and responded to her frantic waving. She looked pale and drawn as she whispered in Marie's ear to give her instructions. Marie slipped away quietly, desperate not to wake Chris. She returned a few minutes later, bringing Sera in tow carrying a bag.

Sera had performed a number of caesareans, but none on a human until the recent unsuccessful attempt. Secretly, she and Kate had discussed this as a measure to be used in desperate circumstances, which she clearly now felt had been met. Sera had been reading medical texts and anatomy studies in preparation, but remained nervous.

The baby was killing Ana, having lost its own battle similarly to Evie. Ana was sedated, and Sera did her best with Kate as the others were sent away quietly.

Dan never knew what happened in there, but neither Kate nor Sera were the same after that.

By some miracle, they saved Ana. She was so badly damaged and exhausted by the process that she remained under for five days. During that time, someone was constantly by her side. Kate had identified the members of the group who had the right blood group; none of them refused to give their own blood to try and keep the young woman alive.

Chris raged in his grief, bellowing like a wounded bull. During the labour it took both Dan and Steve to hold him back, again having to resort to hurting him to keep him from disrupting the medical team trying to save his wife. He collapsed into a heap as all his strength finally deserted him. He lay on the floor and howled as the pain of the news reached every last cell in his body. Dan lay there with him, still holding on to him but no longer in restraint of his powerful frame trying to reach the door.

He slept there on the floor, fitful sobs racking his body intermittently as a toddler would after the fight of the tantrum had left them. When he woke, he was broken. He sat by Ana's side day and night until she woke; then it was her turn to cry and they wept together.

Dan had had his fill of grief. He felt the need to get back out and do something useful, only there was nothing to do. He convinced Steve to take the helicopter out for no real reason other than his own awkwardness at being around the distraught people and his feelings of inactivity.

During the second burial in rapid succession, barely anyone spoke.

JUST LIKE BACK IN 'NAM

Steve was reserved and clearly disappointed about the limited shelf life of their new transport. He made the point, at length, that the expertise needed to keep the machine airworthy was high and sadly extinct as far as he knew. There was plenty of fuel; he estimated about four hours' flight time, and there were numerous small airfields in range. The weather wasn't an issue, he said; these things could fly in minus twenty and in very strong crosswinds.

Dan justified his decision on who to take. He justified it a little too strenuously, clearly defending the fact that he wanted to take his protégé on a helicopter ride. Steve suggested Mitch come too, but recommended that they leave the rest behind to ensure they had carrying capacity for anyone and anything they brought back.

To give a reason for the excursion other than boredom, a list of targets was drawn up given their far extended reach, and Steve worked through flight time and distance and plotted a route to work around refuelling points.

In terms of supplies, the house didn't actually want for much. Mitch suggested some more heavy guns for attaching to the helicopter, whereas Dan was more interested in searching for other survivors.

The plan was to head south and make a thorough search for other survivors while they still had the limited time capability; Steve made it clear almost daily that the helicopter would only do one more trip unless they could find the right fuel. Even if they did, he would only risk a few flights at best without a proper maintenance schedule. Other than what Phil could remember and what Steve knew, they were in the dark, having left the manuals for the aircraft hundreds of miles away.

Steve estimated three hours of searching before visiting a small airfield for a hopeful refuel; if that wasn't possible, there would still be enough juice left to get them home. Everything after that was dependent on them finding the correct fuel.

Over post-breakfast coffee, Leah was given the news that she was coming on a long-range mission. Her mind almost physically began to tick, calculating the kit and supplies she would need to pack. Mitch was in on the joke, presenting her with an aircrew harness and enjoying her confusion.

Her excitement, for once, wasn't hidden. She squealed like the teenager she was and jumped around the office with excitement.

Steve ran through instructions for them all: both side doors would be open and all eyes would be searching for any sign of settlements. He pored over the maps, searching the swathes of farmland for the best places to support people. His last instruction was the most important. "Base layers, windproofs, gloves and hats; it's going to be bloody freezing when we're airborne."

They wrapped up warmly as instructed, so much so that they were all overheating while Phil helped Steve run through the pre-flight checks. Neil looked on with professional interest. An interested crowd braved the cold to watch them take off.

Leah was strapped into the canvas seat nearest the sliding door. Her excitement was palpable, her grin impossibly wide with the fear and anticipation.

She had been on a plane once when she was younger, some wedding abroad paid for by family. She didn't remember it in detail, so in her heart felt that this was the first and probably only time she would ever fly.

Dan strapped in opposite as Mitch showed off by standing and holding on with one hand as the heavy strap dangled to his back. Their weapons were secured tightly and headsets all plugged in.

The heavy bird lifted as it should and gained altitude impossibly fast, surging upwards before Steve tilted the controls. They left, peeling off to the right and heading away from home to quickly leave the crowd in silence. Leah's smile didn't fade at all, but during take off it seemed locked in a rictus of nervous and scared excitement. They craned their necks to see out of the doors and look down on the peaceful landscape. Mitch hooked their safety straps to the loops above the doors and unclipped the tight straps holding them in place.

Very carefully at first, they stood and looked out. The freedom and power Dan felt was incredible; he had ridden in helicopters half a dozen times before during training exercises, but this was something else. As he stared out over the empty landscape, he was overwhelmed by the urge to sit and hang his legs out of the door like he'd seen American soldiers in Vietnam War films do. He mentioned it jokingly into the microphone of his headset.

Steve laughed.

"I wouldn't," he said. "We're doing about a hundred and seventy miles an hour at the moment; it'll suck you out!"

He heard Leah's chuckles over the headset as he stepped back a little further from the open door.

VISITORS FROM ABOVE

They had been in the air for almost an hour before they saw signs of human life.

Steve had slowed and dropped to about four hundred feet to allow time for his passengers to see more clearly. Out of Dan's window, he spotted a moving vehicle and called it out over the headset. Steve turned the big aircraft slowly towards the promise of living people.

Somehow, landing in a helicopter with four armed soldiers made them less cautious than normal. The awe of their arrival should serve to assert their dominance and dissuade any thoughts of hostility; if they had a helicopter, then what else did they have? That was the theory in Dan's mind, anyway. He gave no thought to the fear they would instil in others, or the false hope of a return of order their incredible machine could signify.

The dumbstruck driver of a battered farm 4x4 watched in silence as they swept around in front of him to land. Steve kept the rotors turning as Dan jumped down with Mitch. Leah, for once, didn't pull a face at being told to stay put.

Dan had a quick shouted conversation with the man over the screaming whine of the three screaming engines, gaining his dumbfounded assent to lead them back to the camp. He checked there was enough clear space to land their ride before running low back to the Merlin; it was not strictly necessary, but it didn't hurt to be careful.

It took a few minutes to follow the car back to a large, sprawling farm. Steve made an impressive turn before settling the howling machine on the grass and killing the engines to bathe the shocked survivors in renewed quiet and conserve the remainder of their fuel.

Mitch and Leah stayed to guard the aircraft as fifty or so people came from their work and hiding places to stare at the sudden and overwhelming newcomers. Steve and Dan went into the farmhouse, where they sat with a smaller version of their own leadership council. They were there for almost an hour, having swapped instructions on how to reach each other by road. They numbered only forty and were predominantly farmers. They had suffered badly from an attack last summer and had to resort to using their shotguns for the first time as defensive weapons against other people. It had scarred them deeply, and they promised to discuss with their members about joining Dan's group for companionship and safety.

Leah spoke happily with the villagers who emerged to look at the helicopter, and she received some strange looks about the weapons she carried.

Dan and Steve eventually returned in a subdued mood, shaking hands formally with the elders and wearing uncharacteristically straight faces. They waved as Steve forced the machine off the ground with a backwards motion – so that he could see where he had to put it down if something went wrong during takeoff – and banked away to seek the airfield marked on his map. He gained altitude to use the roads as waypoints and Dan spoke to him while following the map as he sat beside him in the copilot's seat with his hands and feet well away from the controls.

Mitch and Leah exchanged a look but were both too wrapped up in the fun they were having to look too deeply into what their change in mood meant.

The airfield was less than twenty-five minutes' flight away, and the area where the small private helicopters were kept also housed a police helicopter which, Steve said, used the same mix of fuel.

Dan allowed himself a bitter smile looking at the black-and-yellow police chopper; not having been in the air for a year and a half was about par for the course. Unlike a police helicopter, theirs was well equipped to fly in minus twenty degrees Celsius as opposed to being grounded because it was a bit cloudy or the *EastEnders* omnibus was on.

The Merlin was left to cool before the correct fuel was found and carefully pumped into the tanks. Steve reckoned the reserve there was good for a few more days in the air, just as long as he dared to keep flying without the painstaking maintenance required.

Leah was disappointed about the lack of further searching, but Steve declared it was time to head home. Dan barely said a word the whole way back and strode off to the house the second they landed.

EXTINCTION EVENT

He found Marie sitting in Ops, waiting for their return. Ash was with her and his face lit up with excitement at seeing his master return, resulting in a rhythmic thud of his tail on the floor. Dan twitched his head outside and walked back out, unlocking his Discovery and climbing in to warm the engine and flicking both front heated seats to high.

Marie had wrapped up in a large parka and climbed in without a word. He drove. The cab had heated before she said anything.

"Something's pretty bad, isn't it," she said. A statement, not a question.

He slowed and stopped, tiredly flicking the selector into park. He got out and hauled himself onto the bonnet, where he lit a cigarette and breathed deeply.

Laid out in front of him was a crisp, undisturbed landscape.

Marie joined him. "Tell me," she said.

Dan explained about the group they had found, only then realising how perilously close they had been to the former Bronson's reach if they had strayed into the urban areas.

"And?" she prompted, her patience running thin with the mystery revelation she was expecting.

"And they've had three stillbirths with double that in miscarriages," Dan said quietly.

They sat in silence. Their own two could have been a coincidence. For other groups – the villagers and the one that the now dead King of Wales had mentioned – to all have the same issues was too much to accept as mere coincidence; it was a pattern.

Emma's words haunted his mind all day: "We all have it," she had said, but couldn't say how it had left some people alive or what change it had made to them.

"What if Emma is right?" he asked Marie, voicing his thoughts.

For once, she had nothing to say. She hugged his left arm as she sat beside him, resting her head against his shoulder.

"If she's right," she said in a subdued tone, "then this really was our extinction event." She hugged his arm tighter still as her tears began to fall. "It can't be," she said quietly. "I'm having your baby."

EPILOGUE

Leaves blew across the pitted concrete, swirling them up and around inside a large, empty barn. Not strictly empty: the bones and decayed pelts of cattle lay undisturbed save for the scavengers who had long ago picked them clean.

A Land Rover lay on its wheel rims, tyres long weathered away, sitting awkwardly as the green film on it tried to obscure the symbol of vehicular dominance recognised all the world over. Where once the sound of lambs competed with the pigs, chickens and cows, there was now only an eerie silence.

A mile away lay a ruin of concrete, metal and glass. Greenhouses became tin skeletons, as all their glass panels had long since been blown in by the elements. Some were no longer even recognisable, as their contents had grown so tall in their confined space that they looked ridiculous and completely obscured the frames imprisoning them. The wood and plastic sheeting that had made the polytunnels was gone, only the occasional shred of exposed rubbish hinting at what used to be there.

Down the hill from the empty farm, a tree lay strewn across the rough driveway, its branches wilted and leaves gone. The trunk showed signs of rotting, as it had been there through the full turn of seasons.

The grand façade of the beautiful house was streaked with dark green from the blocked and damaged guttering; the once proud solar panels were covered in leaves. Water dripped from cracked glass and pipes, rendering the impressive feat of engineering useless and somehow spoiling the skyline with deformed additions to the architecture. Nature had encroached; thick vines had dug their deep and insidious grip into the stonework, gaining a beachhead on their long campaign to bring the building down and reclaim the materials once stolen to create it.

The large front door lay broken on one side, its hinges gone and the interior opened up to the elements. To the right, the twisted and grotesque remains of a cat lay on the floor under a shelf in a dusty office. To the left, evidence of humans existed in the damaged doorframe, laying bare a room filled with boxes of bullets and the guns to fire them. Thick layers of damp dust had warped and discoloured the cardboard, showing tarnished brass where it was exposed. Peeling paint and collapsed ceilings ran throughout the ground floor, and water dripped incessantly from a dozen obvious leaks. The remnants of what looked like a makeshift hospital lay deserted; cupboards of medicines stood untouched.

A large dining room stood empty and dark, children's drawings now faded and fallen from their places on the walls where they had been displayed. Abandoned cups and plates were strewn across the room which had at one time seen many decisions made and the direction of many lives dictated.

Upstairs, more decay showed as floors creaked and bowed. Rainwater ran down walls, taking paint with it as the inexorability of gravity dragged everything man-made down to the ground.

Back outside, another vehicle was barely visible under the heavy canopy of a willow tree. Strips of what used to be chrome showed up dull in a shaft of light, and all four chunky tyres stood flat and useless.

Once a proud example of status and intent, now just metal and plastic, never to move again.

To the rear of the big house was a lake, although it was overgrown all around and a haven for the teeming wildlife that called it home. Unchecked by predators, the animals ran riot as they competed for the abundant food sources. In the long grass of a field to the side of the lake lay the wreckage of a large machine. Heavy, long blades hung limp where they had not sheared away, and it was impossible to tell whether it was abandoned there or had crashed.

Nature was taking back what once belonged entirely to her; the existence of humans would be erased from this place by the passage of time. The desperate struggle to survive by the last residents would not be documented here, would not be discovered.

A row of small mounds of earth, headstones already long gone, disturbed the continuity of a patch of grass in the sunlight. Perhaps the only evidence of the fight to survive would be found there, one day, long after it happened.

The story continues in AFTER IT HAPPENED BOOK 4: HOPE

A message from the author

Thanks for reading. Please leave a review on Amazon if you enjoyed it!

Also, you can find me on:

Twitter: @DevonFordAuthor

Facebook: Devon C Ford Author

Subscribe to my email list and read my blog:

www.devonfordauthor.uk